Felix Frost
Time Detective

ROMAN RIDDLE

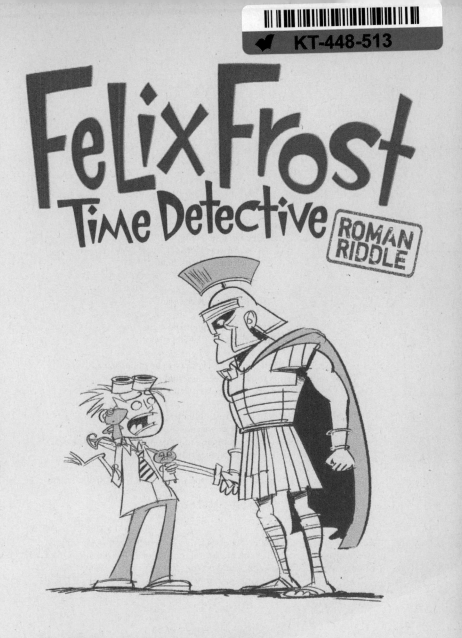

Eleanor Hawken

Quercus

First published in Great Britain in 2015 by
Quercus Publishing Ltd
Carmelite House
50 Victoria Embankment
London EC4Y 0DZ

An Hachette UK company

Text © 2015 Eleanor Hawken
Illustrations © 2015 Steve May

A CIP catalogue record for this book is available from the British Library

PB 978 1 84866 5 606
EBOOK 978 1 84866 8 157

10 9 8 7 6 5 4 3 2 1

Typeset by Tim Rose

Printed and bound in Great Britain by Clays Ltd, St Ives plc

FeLix FrOst
TiMe Detective ROMAN RIDDLE

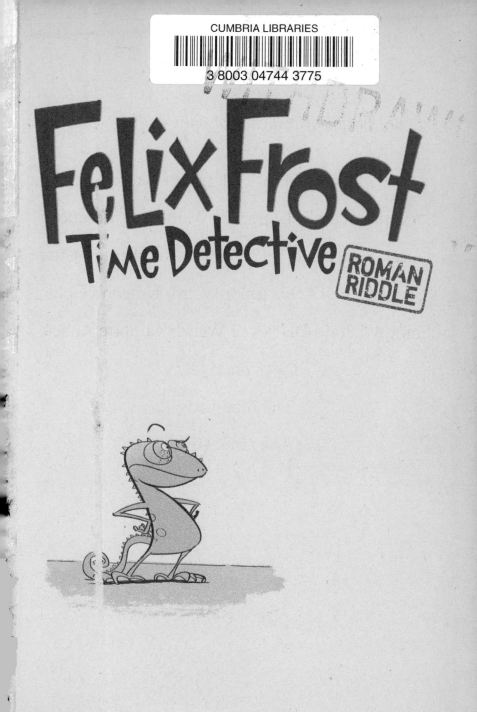

Eleanor Hawken is also the author of

Sammy Feral's Diaries of Weird

Sammy Feral's Diaries of Weird: Yeti Rescue

Sammy Feral's Diaries of Weird: Hell Hound Curse

Sammy Feral's Diaries of Weird: Dragon's Gold

Sammy Feral's Diaries of Weird: Vampire Attack

and

The Blue Lady

The Grey Girl

1

The Accidental Time Machine

Felix Frost put down the soldering iron and whipped off his fireproof gloves. He pushed his safety goggles up over his mop of shaggy brown hair. Wafting away the last wisps of black smoke in the air, he inspected his new invention with pride.

Felix beamed. *This bad boy is going to catapult mankind into the next scientific age.*

Six years in the making and it was finally finished. The teleporter.

Felix's pet chameleon, Einstein, poked his head out of Felix's trouser pocket cautiously. Einstein looked at the teleporter and then up at Felix, who was grinning like a mad clown. The lizard's scales shimmered a deep shade of **orange**. 'There's no need to tell me you're worried, Einstein,' Felix sighed. 'I'm ninety-nine point nine per cent positive this will work. I've done the maths, remember?'

Einstein looked around Felix's small bedroom. Felix followed his gaze. His bookshelves bowed under the weight of advanced physics textbooks and scientific journals. His extensive rock collection was lined up on the top shelf (he'd been fascinated with basic crystal structure since he was five years old). A homemade telescope Felix had used to discover a new planet rested in a corner of the room, and a new species of mould he'd been cultivating in a specimen jar sat by the side of his bed.

That manky mould is going to blast chicken pox into the history books. I just need to put it to the test . . .

The walls were covered in mathematical equations, some of them so old they'd been written in crayon – before Felix had even started school. On the wall next to his bed, Felix had written the dictionary definition of teleportation. It was the first thing he saw every morning when he woke up.

2

$\Delta u = Q - W$

$F = \dfrac{Gm_1 m_2}{r^2}$

$E = mc^2$

Teleportation = the transportation of a physical object from one place to another without it actually travelling from A to B

$T = \sqrt{F} - 2\pi/\omega$

$v_x = v_{0_x} + a_x t$

$x = x_0 + v_{0_x} t + \dfrac{1}{2} a_x t^2$

$v_x^2 - v_{0_x}^2 = 2a_x(x - x_0)$

Schrödinger's Equation

$i\hbar \dfrac{\partial}{\partial t}\psi(r,t) = -\dfrac{\hbar^2}{2m}\nabla^2\psi(r,t) + V(r,t)\psi(r,t)$

One minute you're standing in the kitchen and then, *ZAP*, suddenly you appear on a sunny beach in Spain – that's teleporting.

'People have been teleporting in science fiction since forever ago,' Felix reminded Einstein. 'Harry Potter apparates and disapparates. Dr Who does it, the Power Rangers do it, the weird-looking guys in *Star Trek*, *Stargate* and *X-Men* – they've all done it. And now I'm going to do it too!'

Einstein raised a scaly eyebrow.

'If it's possible in a sci-fi film then it's possible in real life,' Felix said. 'Remember the time I made a scale model of the *Death Star* and levitated it around the room using quantum mechanics and gamma rays?'

Einstein rolled his eyes.

Felix Frost = child genius.

Actually, Felix Frost = secret child genius.

When Felix was three years old he made the mistake of explaining Newton's law of universal gravitation to Missy Six – a girl in his nursery class. She'd jumped off a table, trying to fly. Missy had been taken to hospital with a fractured arm and Felix had been taken to a science lab and had wires attached to his head to see 'what was wrong with him'. Felix's mother managed to convince the scientists that Felix wasn't a genius, that it was all a big misunderstanding. The thing was, Mum had always known her son was 'different', but she didn't want everyone else knowing that. So, as she marched her three-year-old away from the men in white lab coats, she made him promise to keep his genius a secret.

'It's better for everyone that no one understands just how different you are, Felix,' Mum said scornfully. 'Do you want your brain sliced open and used for medical science? Do you want to spend your life in a cage eating nothing but cabbage? And it wouldn't just be you – your father and I, and your brothers, we'd be on the chopping block too you know. Is that what you want, Felix, is it?' Felix quickly shook his head, terrified. 'No, I didn't think so. The longer you can hide your genius, the better.'

From that day on Felix had kept his genius top secret from the world.

The only people who knew were his family.

And they were the only people in the world who could not care less.

'Felix – tea's ready!' Mum bellowed through the house. 'Felix!'

Felix jumped at the sound of his name. 'Mum's been cooking again?' He shuddered at the thought. 'In the name of evolution, if only I could invent myself new taste buds!' Einstein leaped on to the nearby bookshelf, quickly hiding behind a well-thumbed copy of *Advanced Quantum Mechanics*. 'Don't worry, Einstein, I wasn't going to make you eat Mum's food too.'

Einstein peered out between the books. His scales shimmered a puke-like **green**. Felix had trained his pet chameleon to communicate with him by his colour.

Green = disgust
Red = danger
Yellow = happy
Blue = sad
Orange = worry
Purple = yes
Pink = no

Leaving Einstein in the bedroom, Felix headed downstairs and into the kitchen. Felix's mum tutted at the sight of him and ruffled his hair, shaking out a fine layer of coppery dust. 'Have you been playing with your soldering iron again, Felix?' she asked, pushing him towards the kitchen table. 'How many more school shirts are going to go up in flames this year?'

'I'm not playing, Mum.' Felix frowned. 'I've invented a teleporter. Actually, I've just been adding the finishing touches, and after dinner I'm going to—'

'What's for dinner, Mum?' Freddie and Frank burst into the kitchen. 'I'm starving,' they both said in unison. Like every other night of the week, Felix's older brothers had been at football practice. And like every other night of the week, they hadn't bothered to shower before coming home for dinner.

'Don't you guys ever use the super-strength stink-eradicator spray I made you?' Felix pinched his nose at their smell. 'If it's run out I can easily rustle up some more. All I have to do is break down the chemical structure of normal deodorant and then rebuild the molecules with—'

'Good football practice?' Their dad strode into the kitchen and took his place at the top of the table. 'Sorry I wasn't there to watch today,' he apologized. 'I sat in traffic for over two hours on the way back from work. All the roads at the top of town are closed off.'

'Why?' Felix asked.

'The radio said something about a body being dug up in an old woman's garden,' Dad mumbled.

'WHAT?' Felix's mum waved a spatula about in the air in horror. 'A body! Buried in a garden! Will we be next? Murdered in our beds and—'

'Calm down.' Felix's dad shook his head. 'The body's thousands of years old. Roman apparently.'

'Who cares about some mouldy old Roman?' Freddie frowned. 'Guess who scored a hat trick at practice, Dad?'

Dad beamed. 'Tell me all about it, son.'

Freddie nodded and launched into a blow-by-blow description of how he'd scored the winning goal with a single strike from the far end of the pitch, while their mum dished up brown slop on to everyone's plates.

Why is it that I can name every element in the periodic table but I can't think of one thing I have in common with any of my family? Felix thought, pushing a blob of brown mush around his plate. *If it wasn't for those DNA tests I ran on Mum's and Dad's hair then I'd be convinced I was swapped at birth.*

'I've got the highest goal-scoring record in the school,' Freddie boasted, lifting another mouthful of slop to his smirking mouth.

'I'm only one goal behind,' Frank quickly pointed out.

'We're all very proud of you.' Mum smiled.

'Are you listening to this, Felix?' Dad asked. 'Maybe one day you'll be more like your brothers.'

Felix looked down at his plate. 'Maybe.'

After dinner Felix escaped to the sanctuary of his bedroom. He closed the door behind him and sighed deeply. 'Sometimes I think you're the only creature in the world who understands me,' he said to Einstein. 'I've probably got more in common with a Roman skeleton than my family.' Felix reached into his pocket. 'Here, I brought something for you.'

Einstein swiftly flashed a shocking shade of **green**.

'Don't worry – it isn't the brown sludge I had to eat.' Felix pulled out a limp lettuce leaf, and Einstein's scales shimmered a warm **yellow** as he nibbled hungrily on it.

Felix turned to the teleporter and smiled.

Felix had used an old microwave to create the first part of the teleporter. He'd carefully taken the microwave apart, rewired it and replaced the internal computer with a more sophisticated engine that he'd designed himself. The microwave no longer heated food – it shot out powerful laser beams that could deconstruct the atoms in any object. Felix had removed the microwave door and angled the lasers so they shot out of the machine and hit whatever was standing in front of it.

'Just one more thing to do before it's time to switch on this bad boy . . .' Felix took out his old Swiss army knife from his pocket, flicked it open and put the blade to the side of the microwave. He carved his signature on to the side.

TF

The same signature Felix had carved on to all his greatest scientific inventions.

Felix picked up his Yoda action figure from his bedside table. 'Yoda,' Felix said to his favourite childhood toy, 'you've been there for all the mega moments of my life. The time I broke the speed of sound with my nuclear catapult. The time I launched my homemade rocket. The time I made radioactive slime using the contents of Mum's cleaning cupboard. Now you get to go where no man, lizard or action figure has ever gone before.' He carefully placed Yoda in the firing line of the old microwave's lasers.

'Once the laser beams hit Yoda, his atoms will blast apart and he'll completely disappear,' Felix reminded Einstein. 'But a split second later, his atoms will reconstruct themselves and Yoda will pop up over here . . .' Felix walked over to the other side of the room, where the second part of the teleporter sat. Felix had built it out of an old oven hotplate. 'And then Yoda will have successfully teleported from one side of the room to the other.' Felix grinned madly. 'The time has come to make history!'

Felix looked over at Einstein, who let out a burp of appreciation as he finished the soggy lettuce leaf. 'You're the only one here to witness this historic moment, Einstein. Get comfortable.' Einstein began to climb up on to a higher shelf to get a better view. Or run for cover. Felix couldn't be sure.

Felix pulled his safety goggles down over his

eyes. He picked up the old TV remote that he'd rewired to control the teleporter, and tapped in the particle wave frequency he needed: 0061.

Then he punched in the laser heat (56) and intensity (41).

His finger hovered above the green button.

Einstein took his place on the top bookshelf, among Felix's rock collection. In the corner of his eye Felix caught a glimpse of Einstein's scales flashing a worried **orange**. Determined, Felix lowered his finger towards the green button.

'Yoda, may the force be with you.'

Einstein flinched backward, knocking into a piece of smoky quartz. As Felix pressed down on the green button, the rock tumbled from the shelf, falling directly into the path of the laser beam.

'No! Wait!' Felix reached out, trying to catch the rock.

But it was too late.

A blue laser shot out of the old microwave, hitting the small piece of quartz. The rock spun madly in the air, held in place by the force of the laser beam pulsing through it. The laser hummed and crackled like a light sabre, travelling through the rock and heading straight for Yoda.

Felix held his breath as the blue laser blasted Yoda.

Yoda began to fade away in front of Felix's eyes . . .

'Eureka! I've done it!' Felix pushed up his goggles and looked at the old oven plate on the other side of his bedroom. 'Even though the rock got in the way of the laser it didn't matter. Yoda's disappeared! Wow! Bullseye! Home run! Back of the net! Check out Yoda blasting back into existence just over . . .'

But the oven plate was empty.

'Any second now . . .' Felix muttered in anticipation. 'Any second . . .'

One second later . . . two seconds . . . three . . .

The seconds stretched into minutes.

Yoda didn't reappear. He had vanished into thin air.

Felix scratched his messy brown hair. 'Impossible. Atoms can't just disappear. Energy can't just disappear. Everyone knows that! Yoda must have gone somewhere . . .'

Felix ran frantically towards a set of equations scrawled over his bedroom wall. His eyes darted over them as he traced the numbers and letters with his fingers. 'If X is divided by the square root of Y, and that is set off by the heat of the laser . . . I'm right . . . I know I am . . . this should work . . . this HAS worked. Yoda has disappeared – I just don't know where he's disappeared to . . . If that stupid rock hadn't fallen down and sent Yoda spinning off who knows where . . .'

Einstein leaped off the bookshelf on to Felix's

shoulder. His scales glowed a fierce **red** – he knew what Felix was thinking.

'Don't try to stop me, Einstein,' Felix warned his pet lizard, walking towards the piece of smoky quartz that had fallen to the ground. 'This bit of pesky rock,' he held it up, 'holds the key to getting Yoda back.' Einstein's scales were the colour of burning coals now. 'Just who do you think I am, Einstein?' Felix asked, his eyes alight with adventure. 'The kind of friend who would abandon a companion to an unknown fate? The kind of scientist who won't stop at nothing to discover the truth? NO! I am Felix Frost! Inventor, adventurer – and I am going after him . . .'

Felix held the quartz rock in one hand and the remote control in the other. He looked down at the green button, quickly calculating the risks involved in putting himself in the line of fire:

✳ *I could be teleported a thousand miles away.*

✳ *I could be teleported to another planet, in another galaxy, in another universe . . .*

✳ *I could be killed.*

He weighed up the danger.

He knew the risks.

He didn't care.

Felix tapped the wave frequency into the remote control. He pulled his safety goggles back down, took a deep breath and stood in the path of the laser beam.

'In the name of science . . . Let's rock 'n' roll!'

Felix tossed the rock into the air and pressed down on the green button firmly. He held his breath as the laser beam blasted out of the microwave, hitting the rock and suspending it in mid-air.

The bright blue laser pulsed through the rock and slammed into Felix's body with the force of a stun gun.

It was as if he had swallowed a nuclear bomb and it had detonated inside him.

Fire rushed through his veins as every part of Felix blasted apart into a billion pieces. Every hair on his head was plucked out, his skin pulling away from his bones, his bones tearing away from his muscles – every vein and tissue inside of him blasted out into the unknown.

The world around Felix melted away. The equations on his bedroom walls, his stacks of physics textbooks, the old microwave – everything that was familiar to him disappeared and his vision was flooded with darkness.

Every atom of Felix's body began to hurtle through space and time . . .

Before Felix could formulate a single theory about what had happened, he felt every particle suddenly being squashed back together. As though he were nothing more than a human-shaped elastic band that had been stretched beyond recognition and quickly snapped back into place.

Destroyed and rebuilt in a nanosecond.

The world began to glimmer back into existence – but everything was different. Instead of his bedroom walls and unmade bed, Felix could see vast stone buildings and marble statues. Instead of the faint murmur of the TV coming from downstairs, he could hear the chatter of hundreds of people rushing past him. He could feel fresh air on his face, and smell the stench of unwashed bodies and heavy incense wafting on the breeze. What looked like a Roman centurion marched straight past him.

'What in Newton's name . . .'

One thing was certain. Felix was alive. And he was back in one piece.

'Einstein,' Felix whispered in horror, pushing his goggles up into his bird-nest hair so he could get a better look. His hands and feet stung with pins and needles as his body knitted itself back together. 'What have I done . . . ? And where in galloping galaxies have I taken us?'

2
The March of the Gladiators

'Yoda!'

With Einstein still on his shoulder, Felix sank to his hands and knees and crawled towards his trusty action figure, which had been kicked into the gutter of the dusty street. Dozens of sandal-clad feet scurried past without glancing down at the small plastic toy, which looked ridiculously out of place.

He picked up the action figure and clutched it to his thumping chest as if Yoda could somehow save him. 'You're OK,' Felix muttered to the plastic object.

Where in Newton's name am I? he quickly thought. *Some kind of film set maybe?*

Felix's eyes followed a pair of filthy feet as they

hurried past. A man's feet. White material swung around his ankles, the bottom of which was covered with dirt and dust. *Wow, that's a very detailed costume . . .*

The man slipped through the bustling crowd and disappeared from sight. That's when Felix noticed that everyone around him was dressed in similar costumes. Lengths of material wrapped around their bodies, fastened with buckles and pins, some with coloured sashes worn over one shoulder. *Togas*, Felix realized. *Romans.*

Pulling himself up on wobbly legs, Felix gazed around in amazement. He was in a vast square. Colossal stone buildings surrounded him on every side, each building flanked by huge marble pillars and carved with Roman numerals and Latin words. To his right was a large statue of an important-looking man in a toga. A name was engraved on to the statue's base: '**NERO CLAUDIUS CAESAR AUGUSTUS GERMANICUS**'.

Wow, this film set is immense . . .

Felix looked around again, expecting to see a rig of lights and film cameras, and the director sitting in a canvas chair. But all he saw were more buildings, statues and people bustling about – and a man walking towards him. He was wearing an old grey toga covered with rips and stains. By his side were two small children, their faces encrusted with dirt, their hair matted. They held out bowls in front of them, begging the people rushing past for food.

Behind them strode a man wearing metal armour over a red tunic, and a helmet with red bristles poking upward towards the sky.

Winking wormholes! That really is the best Roman centurion costume I've ever seen!

Felix watched as the centurion marched up to the old man and two children, and pulled a shining sword out of the sheath tied to his waist. It glinted in the sunlight.

Only a solid metal surface can reflect light that way, Felix noted. *An alloy of iron and carbon maybe? Steel? That's not a prop sword . . . it's a real sword . . . wowsers!*

'Excuse me!' Felix called out at the top of his voice.

The Roman centurion did a double take at Felix pushing through the crowd. He lowered his sword and the old man and two children quickly scurried away.

'Excuse me,' Felix said again, walking right up to the centurion. 'Are you a main character in the film? Or just an extra? That's an impressive sword – do you all have one?'

'In Nero's name, get out of here,' the soldier snarled at Felix. 'Or I'll have you chained up and whipped for a week.'

'I'm not part of the film.' Felix shook his head. 'I'm not meant to be here at all actually.'

The soldier stared intently at Felix. His eyes travelled up and down – studying his scuffed school shoes, his black trousers and singed school shirt, not to mention the lizard sat on his shoulder and the plastic toy clutched to his chest.

'Slave,' the soldier said slowly. 'Who is your master?'

Felix chuckled. 'Is this what movie stars call "method acting"? Staying in character when the cameras stop rolling? Impressive, but I really should get going. Umm, where's the exit?'

'If you run from me, boy . . .' The soldier took a menacing step towards Felix. Fury flashed through the man's eyes like a bolt of thunder. '. . . I'll have you recaptured and thrown to the lions. Come willingly and you'll only receive forty lashes.'

Once again Felix looked around for the light rigs, the catering trailers, the sound boom and the director, and once again all he saw were Roman citizens.

Something's not right here . . .

He stepped backward, his feet stumbling in the gutter.

Felix felt Einstein scurry down his arm and hide away in his trouser pocket. He didn't need to see the lizard to know he was glowing **red** for danger.

Something is very, very wrong . . .

A horrible realization suddenly dawned upon him.

When the quartz rock fell into the path of the laser it somehow changed the way the teleporter works . . . now it doesn't just move an object through space, it moves it through space AND TIME!

Felix's breathing sped up and he felt a bead of sweat begin to trickle down his face.

The digits I tapped into the remote control . . . the particle wave frequency, the laser heat and intensity . . .

The year was 0061.

The co-ordinates were 56 and 41.

THE TELEPORTER HAS TIME TRAVELLED ME TO ANCIENT ROME!

Reality crashed down around Felix like the weight of a galaxy.

'I've created a time machine,' Felix blurted out. The soldier gripped the hilt of his sword and narrowed his eyes at Felix.

'Slave,' the soldier growled, 'your backside will be red for a whole month when I've finished with you!' He turned around and shouted to a large group of what Felix now knew with absolute certainty and terror were Roman soldiers. 'Capture this slave!'

'Einstein!' Felix stepped backward, away from the large group of soldiers who stared at him, reaching for their swords. 'They're speaking Latin! But I can understand! Why . . . ?' Felix felt Einstein's claws sink into the top of his thigh. 'You're right,' Felix whispered to Einstein. 'That is not what I should be worrying about right now. Right now I need to—'

'Seize him!' shouted the first soldier. 'In Nero's name I command you to stop!' Felix's grip tightened around Yoda as his feet kicked up the dust on the busy street and began to sprint across the cobbles. He had no idea where he was going, he just knew he had to escape.

'Stop that slave!' the first soldier cried, chasing Felix through the busy square.

'I'm wearing a school uniform, not slave shackles!' Felix screamed over his shoulder, darting between the crowds. He elbowed his way past a fat man carrying a pile of scrolls, past a young girl selling flowers, past a woman screaming at a small child. He ducked down as he ran between two men carrying a large crate of chickens, and leaped over an old man bending to buckle his sandal. There wasn't time to stop and take in the sights and smells of Ancient Rome, no time to think about the enormity of what he had done. *Run from the men with swords*, was all Felix could think. *Run far, far away . . .*

Felix knocked into a woman carrying a basket on her head. The basket fell to the ground and oranges spilled out into the street. Felix dared to glance behind him and saw a couple of the soldiers trip over the rolling oranges, skidding and falling flat on the ground.

But there were still two more soldiers following him. Each had their sword unsheathed and pointed at Felix.

Felix felt Einstein's claws sink deeper into his flesh as he hurtled through the street. Felix barged through a group of fat toga-wearing men, who called after him as he ran: 'Delinquent! Crook! Rotten pleb! Stinking cockroach!'

Felix chanced another glance over his shoulder, hoping he'd managed to lose the chasing soldiers. No such luck.

'You'll be thrown in with the lions when we catch you, slave!' cried the angry soldier at his heels.

Felix took a sharp right, running underneath a large marble arch. He found himself in the middle of a busy market.

He blinked at the bustling crowds as it dawned on him: *I'm never going to lose the soldiers — they know these streets, not me. I need to outwit them . . . trick them . . . hide in plain sight.*

He darted desperately through the people, his eyes scanning for something to help him hide.

Felix spotted a market stall selling cloth on the far side of the market square. **Perfect!** Felix sprinted the last few metres. The cloth merchant was proudly stretching out lengths of red silk, showing them off to a haughty-looking woman. Felix ran straight past and tugged the fabric free from the merchant's sweaty grasp. 'Sorry!' Felix shouted as he ran away, the red cloth wrapping around him. The man waved an angry fist at Felix, but Felix didn't stick around to hear his furious shouts.

Oh Batman's boxer shorts, they're still right behind me!

There was a small, dark alleyway to the left. He darted down it, jumping over stinking piles of rotten fruit and broken baskets, the sound of the market fading from earshot as he ran. At the end of the alleyway he could see a gaggle of children walking along the street. They were all dressed in red togas – just like his.

A school trip! Felix thought hopefully, running towards them. *Thank Andromeda! I can hide among them . . .*

Felix pulled the top of his red toga up over his face as he forged his way into the group of children.

His safety goggles were still sitting on the top of his head – he quickly pulled strands of unruly hair over to hide them. Felix glanced back and saw the Roman soldiers run out of the alleyway and look around, confused.

Thank the cosmos . . . I've lost them, for now . . .

Felix tried to catch his breath. He felt someone tug on his toga and looked to see a small blond boy smiling at him.

'I've never seen you before,' the boy said.

'Of course you haven't,' Felix said, thinking quickly. 'I just joined the school today.'

'Wow.' The boy looked impressed. 'You must be really good if they're already letting you come along.'

Felix's back straightened a little. 'I am that good actually. In fact I'm top of my class.'

The boy gulped nervously. 'Well, we'll be there soon.'

Felix nodded as if he knew exactly what the boy was talking about. As they walked through the streets, away from the market, Felix looked around at the other children. Wherever they were heading to obviously wasn't that exciting – not one of them was smiling. If anything they looked worried. Very worried.

'Err . . . remind me where it is we're going?' Felix asked the blond boy.

The boy looked at Felix as if he had just sprouted another head. 'Nero's Games, of course.'

'Nero's Games?' Felix repeated.

Felix mentally sifted his way through all the information stored in his head until he found something, anything that could help him . . .

✳ **Nero** = a Roman emperor who ruled from 54–68 AD

✳ **Random Nero fact** = he murdered his mother and two wives

✳ **Games** = include gladiator combat, chariot racing

'Watching gladiators fight to the death?' Felix smiled at the boy. 'I can think of worse ways to spend a Thursday evening.'

The group turned a corner and Felix gawped at the ginormous stone building up ahead.

'We're here,' said the boy, pointing at the building.

Jumping Jupiter . . .

The building was a huge elliptical amphitheatre, over ten storeys tall. **Wow.** Thousands of people queued up outside, and Felix could hear the cheering from those who had already taken their seats inside the arena. **Must be a pretty important fight they've all come to see,** he thought.

Instead of queuing up with the crowds, a guard led the group of children to the side of the building, down a narrow alleyway and through a heavy wooden gate. The gate shook and pulsed as the roar of the crowd grew louder and louder. It was the sound of thousands of bloodthirsty spectators, hungry for the games and slaughter to begin. They were chanting in unison – Felix could just about make out some of the words.

'ATTILIUS! ATTILIUS! BLOOD AND GLORY BE HIS NAME.

ATTILIUS! ATTILIUS! SMITE AND BLOW AND MAIM.

ATTILIUS! ATTILIUS! SLAUGHTERER OF BABES.

ATTILIUS! ATTILIUS! GOLDEN HELMET, SHINING BLADE.'

A feeling of unease began to creep through Felix's veins, and he shifted his weight from one foot to another. 'Why are we here behind this gate?' Felix asked the boy. 'Why aren't we sitting in the arena with everyone else?'

'You don't know?' The boy looked surprised.

It was at that moment that Felix realized travelling back in time was the worst thing he had ever done. Worse even than when he'd accidentally set his bedroom on fire while experimenting with an earlier model of the teleporter.

Felix looked around at the group of children. Some of them were crying. Others closed their eyes and muttered words of prayer, their knees knocking against each other.

Felix mentally checked off their facial expressions:

* *Widened eyes.*
* *Eyebrows slanted upward.*
* *Shallow breathing.*
* *Perspiration around temples.*

'You're scared,' Felix said to the boy.

The boy looked up at him. 'Of course I am. You might be the best in your class, but aren't you scared too?'

'Why would I be scared?' Felix asked, though he dreaded the boy's answer. 'We're here to watch the games.'

'We're not here to watch the games,' answered the boy. 'We *are* the games. By the time the sun sets on Rome, we'll all be dead.'

3

Lambs to the Slaughter

Dead by sunset?! Jumping Jupiter!

The children were jostled forward, towards the arena entrance. Felix found his feet shuffling in the same direction, swept along with the crowd. 'Er, excuse me!' he shouted out to anyone who would listen. 'There's been a terrible mistake. I shouldn't be here. Excuse me . . .' He turned around and tried to push his way back through the crowd of children. But it was like swimming against a strong tide.

'I thought you said you were here for the games,' called the blond-haired boy. 'You said you were the best in your class – you said—'

'Yes, I know what I said,' Felix snapped back,

moving around to face the boy and once again being swept along with the current of children. 'But the correlation between the things people say and the truth isn't always accurate.'

'Huh?' the boy replied. 'What's your name?'

'Felix.'

The boy nodded his head in approval. 'That's a strong Roman name. Funny – because you speak Latin with a strange accent, I thought you might be from one of the colonies. I'm Lucius.'

'Well, Lucius,' Felix said, trying not to panic. 'You need to help me. There's been a mistake. I shouldn't be here. And yes, I do speak Latin with a strange accent – do you know why? It's because I shouldn't be speaking it at all. I'm not even sure why I can speak Latin. I can only assume that when my molecules were blasted apart and spat out here in Ancient Rome they reassembled in a way that made me understand the native language.'

'Have you been hit over the head one too many times in the gladiator training ground?' Lucius frowned.

'I've never even stepped foot in a training

ground,' Felix tried to explain calmly, even though he was feeling very far from calm. 'Never swung a punch, or even had to duck one. I've spent my whole life trying to blend in. I've never been in a fight! Don't you understand – I SHOULDN'T BE HERE!'

'None of us should be here.' Lucius shook his head. 'Most kids get to train in gladiator school until they're at least eighteen before they're thrown into the arena to fight. Even then, newly qualified gladiators start off with easy fights. Starved slaves, half-dead hippos – that kind of thing. Not someone like Attilius.'

'Attilius?'

'Attilius,' Lucius replied seriously, as if the word alone should strike fear into Felix's heart. Felix looked at Lucius with a blank expression. 'Are you sure you're not from one of the colonies? Or have you been living under a large rock your whole life?'

No, thought Felix. *I live in a house two thousand years into the future.*

'Who hasn't heard of Attilius?'

'Attilius! Attilius! Golden helmet, shining blade . . .' Felix muttered, remembering the words chanted by the bloodthirsty crowd.

'Exactly! Attilius – the most brutal gladiator who's ever lived. He's never lost a fight. And Emperor Nero thinks it will be funny to watch us all fight him. We're not even allowed weapons.' Lucius held up his empty hands.

'Funny?!' Felix spluttered. 'Galloping Galileo! Whoopee cushions are funny. People who can't understand calculus are funny. My wonky little toe is funny. Killing children is NOT funny.'

'Try telling Nero that.' Lucius looked around furtively, checking that no one was listening to their conversation. 'Talking badly about the emperor gets you an automatic death sentence . . .'

'Well that's hardly something to worry about seeing as we've only got about five minutes to live anyway,' Felix pointed out.

Lucius was careful to say his next sentence very quietly. 'I heard Nero had his own mother killed because he thought it would be the ultimate practical joke. I think he's also had his wife killed and—'

'Emperor Nero is a nutcase.' Felix nodded. 'He's loopier than the far arm of the galaxy on a stormy day. There's no way he'll just let us walk out of here alive. We need to escape!'

'Why would you want to escape?' Lucius frowned.

'Er, why *wouldn't* I? You might not be planning to see your next birthday, but I am. How am I ever going to grow up to be a famous scientist if I die here today?'

'I want to be a farmer,' Lucius sighed. 'I guess dreams don't always come true. I'd be a farmer now if my family hadn't sold me into slavery.'

Wow. And I thought my family were mean . . .

Lucius thrust his left fist in Felix's face. A heavy-looking gold ring on Lucius's little finger glinted in the sunlight. 'See this?' Lucius pointed to the ring. 'That's my family ring. Two hawks flying in circles.'

'Attilius! Attilius!'

The sound of the crowd beyond the gate was getting louder. It could only mean one thing. The gates were about to swing open and the fight was about to start.

Felix looked around desperately, searching for some means of escape.

'Not every family has a family ring . . .' Lucius said wistfully.

Felix shot Lucius an exasperated glare. *I really don't have time to hear your life story . . .*

'My family were once one of the most powerful families in Rome. We owned most of the farmland to the north of the city. We had a huge house – mosaic floors, family shrines, all sorts. But when Nero raised taxes to pay for more statues of himself around the city my family became bankrupt. They had no choice but to sell one of us into slavery. I'm their youngest son – so it makes sense that it was me they had to sell.'

Felix frowned deeply. *It makes no sense at all!*

'Ever since I left home I've been dreaming of this moment,' Lucius said in a whisper so quiet Felix could barely hear him above the roar of the crowd. 'In my dreams I walk into the arena to the sound of my name and then I defeat Attilius barehanded. If I win I'll be a legend. They'll call me "Lucius the Giant Slayer". They'll build statues of me, sing songs about me. People will name their firstborn sons after me and my parents will welcome me back home with open arms.'

I've never heard of a gladiator called Lucius the Giant Slayer in any history book.

The crowd inside the arena let out an almighty roar, rattling the heavy wooden gates in their hinges.

'It's time,' Lucius whispered. He turned to Felix. 'For the glory of the Empire. May the gods be with you.'

People stopped believing in Roman gods thousands of years ago, Felix thought, his heart racing. *I may as well ask a field of cabbages for help right now . . .*

The gates slowly creaked open, pulled apart by two thick-armed Roman centurions. Felix caught his first glimpse of the arena beyond. It was as large as a football pitch, and rows of stone seats towered into the sky. Thousands of spectators jumped up and down with excitement. An almighty roar filled his ears and a thousand fists pumped in the air as the chant of 'ATTILIUS! ATTILIUS! ATTILIUS!' grew louder and louder.

Across the arena, sitting on a golden throne glinting in the midday sun, was a fat man with a crown of golden leaves on his head and a heavy purple toga draped across his body. Two small slave children fanned him with golden palm leaves from either side. His fat face creased into a smug grin as he saw the group of terrified child gladiators being ushered into the arena. He shoved a handful of nuts towards his face, some landing in his mouth and others falling to the ground.

'Let me guess,' Felix whispered to Lucius. 'That's Nero.'

But Lucius didn't answer back – his gaze was fixed on another gate on the far side of the arena, next to Nero. As the gate was pulled open by Roman soldiers, out of it burst a golden chariot containing what looked like a giant.

The chariot was pulled by two bulls, its wheels bigger than Felix.

The crowd went wild.

'ATTILIUS! ATTILIUS! ATTILIUS!'

Attilius waved his arms in the sky. In one hand he held a large metal axe, and in the other a solid golden shield. His body was covered from head to toe in thick metal armour, and on his head he wore a shining gold helmet. The helmet completely covered his head and face, with only two narrow slits for eyes. Above the two eye slits was an intricate engraving of a man carrying a sword in one hand and an axe in the other. Felix noticed that Attilius's shield was also engraved with the figure of a man, although this man looked different from the one on the helmet. The man on the shield held a club in his right hand.

'If we're going to fight this beast then we need a

weapon,' Felix said, hearing the desperation in his voice.

'No weapons allowed,' Lucius said in a small croak.

This isn't a fight, thought Felix. *It's lambs to the slaughter.*

'Silence!' boomed a low voice.

Felix looked across the arena – Emperor Nero had stood up and the crowd fell silent as he spoke. 'Today Rome will witness one of the greatest games ever played. Today Attilius fights for his freedom. If he manages to slaughter every child in the arena before the sand falls in the hourglass, then he will be a free man. If he does not, then he will fight again tomorrow, and again the next day and the next.'

Nero lifted an hourglass in front of him, filled with golden sand.

'One . . . two . . . three!' The crowd erupted into a chorus of cheers as Nero flipped over the hourglass and the sand began to fall.

Felix felt Lucius take a step forward, offering himself up as the first child to fight Attilius.

Before Felix could stop himself, he'd grabbed

hold of Lucius's toga, pulled him back and taken his place at the front of the pack. Another child shoved Felix further forward, and he was suddenly standing out from the crowd, alone in the arena, ready to face his death.

The crowd held their breath as the huge figure of Attilius slowly climbed down from his chariot.

He pointed his axe towards Felix before lifting it up and swinging it in wild circles. The sound of the axe cutting through the air chilled Felix to the core.

I've never even fought my brothers before.

I can't throw a punch . . .

I can't even run that fast . . .

I have no weapons . . .

No training . . .

No hope . . .

Felix took a steady breath. *Is this really how I die? In a gladiator arena in Ancient Rome?*

That's when he felt something move in his toga.

Einstein!

Einstein was tugging on something in Felix's pocket.

The time machine remote control!

Felix had completely forgotten about it.

As Attilius began to run towards him, his axe high and ready to strike, Felix reached between the folds of his toga, into his trouser pocket, and pulled out the remote control.

Co-ordinates . . . 51.6, 0.15. Year: 2015.

His shaking finger jammed down on the green button.

The jeering Roman crowd began to melt away before his eyes. He felt a scorching energy blast every cell in his body apart, and the wind rushed at his face as though he were hurtling through the Earth's atmosphere, zooming at hundreds of miles an hour. His stomach tightened and he felt bile rise up his throat. Just as he thought he was about to vomit his feet landed with a thud on his bedroom floor.

Without thinking Felix bolted towards his door.

Felix flew down the stairs and into his family living room, still draped in his red toga.

'Mum, Dad,' he panted. 'I'm back. I'm alive!'

His mum briefly looked up from a crossword in a glossy magazine before returning her attention to it without a word.

'Freddie!' Felix shouted. 'Frank!'

'Felix, move out of the way,' Frank complained. 'I can't see the TV.'

'How long have I been gone for?' Felix said, wide-eyed. 'Hours, days?'

'Felix, what are you talking about?' Freddie said. 'We saw you five minutes ago at dinner. And what are you wearing? I swear you get weirder every day.'

Felix looked down at the red material wrapped over his clothes, and the remote control he held in his shaking hand. 'Um, sorry . . . forget I said anything . . .' he mumbled, turning to leave.

'Already forgotten,' he heard his dad say as he left the room.

Felix scratched his head as he climbed the stairs to his bedroom.

'So I can travel thousands of years into the past, stay there for hours and then come back to the moment I left . . .'

Felix felt Einstein crawl out of his trouser pocket, up his body, along his arm and out on to his hand. The lizard sat on the remote control and tapped his foot over the red button.

'Don't worry, Einstein,' Felix said, his voice quivering. 'I won't use the time machine ever again. Ever.'

4
The Golden Helmet

Felix hid the time machine, the remote control and the red toga under his bed.

He couldn't sleep at all that night. All he could think about was the time machine under his bed and the children he'd left behind to face a certain and brutal death.

Lucius died two thousand years ago, he told himself. *There's nothing I can do. I can't change the past . . . well, I could change the past, I have a time machine . . . but it would be wrong, wouldn't it?*

* * *

'What should I do, Einstein?' Felix wondered out loud the next morning, as he tightened his school tie in

49

the mirror. 'Should I tell the Royal Scientific Society? Write a paper about my accidental time machine and publish it to worldwide acclaim? Should I go back in time and try to save Lucius? Or just leave the old microwave under the bed and never touch it ever again?'

Einstein flashed **purple**: yes.

'Maybe pretending yesterday never happened would be for the best,' Felix agreed. 'Want to come to school with me today?' Einstein changed to bright pink: no.

The school day was a total write-off.

Double science was Felix's last lesson of the day. Mrs Banks stood in front of the whiteboard and droned on about the science of quicksand.

Felix rubbed at his tired eyes.

I used cornflour and water to make my own quicksand in the bath when I was three years old! I was stuck there for a whole day before Dad agreed to cut me out. I'd rather be back at Nero's Games fighting Attilius than listen to this brain-bending bore!

'Pay attention, class. There are four key ingredients to quicksand.' Mrs Banks scribbled on the board. 'Sand, water, clay and salt.'

Paying attention was the last thing Felix could do. A million and one questions whizzed around his brain like electrons in a nuclear reactor . . . *What have I done? Is time travel the best thing or the worst thing to ever be invented? Should I use the machine again? Should I tell someone? Who would I tell . . . ?*

Felix looked around at the other children in his science class. There was no one he trusted. No one knew that he was a genius. *Looks like I'm in this alone.*

This included Derek and Syd – Felix's so-called 'best friends' – who sat next to Felix at the back of the class, also paying no attention to Mrs Banks. They had known Felix for years and had never thought it was odd that he hadn't invited them to his house.

There's no way I can risk having them there. One look at Felix's bedroom walls would have exposed him for the secret freak he was.

Derek and Syd knew as much about Felix as they did about astrophysics. Absolutely nothing.

'Psst, Felix,' whispered Derek. 'Check this out . . .' Derek shoved a little finger deep into his nostril and scooped out a large wet bogie. Both Derek and Syd erupted into a fit of giggles.

'Flick it, go on,' Syd chuckled, doing a terrible job of keeping his voice down. Mrs Banks's eyes narrowed towards the back of the room and she caught Felix staring at her.

'Felix, pay attention please,' Mrs Banks muttered, turning back to the whiteboard.

'Go on, flick it,' Syd encouraged Derek.

Derek put the fresh bogie on the palm of his hand and then flicked it as far as he could. It soared out of sight.

'Where's it gone?' Syd looked around.

Darwin's beard! thought Felix, trying not to roll his eyes. **It's hardly difficult to work out! From the force Derek used to flick it, and the estimated weight of the bogie, it must have travelled . . .**

'Ughh! Gross!' screamed a girl in the row in front of them. She leaped from her chair, threw her school blazer to the ground and pointed to the large blob of green snot that was sitting on her shiny prefect badge. 'Exactly which zoo did you escape from?' She glared at Felix.

'That's enough, Missy,' Mrs Banks said. 'Sit back down.'

Missy didn't sit back down. She stood and stared at Felix, her blonde corkscrew curls framing her angry face.

Missy Six = Felix's arch nemesis.

Ever since that fateful day in nursery school when Missy had broken her arm jumping off of a table, Missy had been obsessed with one thing.

Felix Frost was a secret genius – and she was going to prove it.

Missy couldn't understand anyone who wanted to hide how clever they were. Missy wore her 'Class Prefect' and 'Science Club Captain' badges on her school blazer with pride. Everyone knew how smart Missy was, and she wasn't in the least bit ashamed.

'Felix.' Mrs Banks pointed at him. 'Seeing as you don't feel you need to listen in class, I assume that means you already know everything there is to know about quicksand.'

'Of course he does.' Missy folded her arms over her chest.

Of course I do!

'Missy, sit down.' Missy dropped back into her chair, her eyes never leaving Felix.

'Is it possible to rescue

someone from quicksand?' Mrs Banks asked Felix.

Felix shrugged. 'I have no idea,' he lied.

Mrs Banks smiled smugly. 'I didn't think so, Felix. Please pay attention from now on. Right,' she turned back to the whiteboard, 'Daniel Bonn's measurements show us that—'

'You'd need a force of ten thousand Newtons just to extract a trapped foot,' Felix mouthed to himself.

'What was that, Felix?' Missy said loudly. 'What was that about Newtons?'

Oh, for the love of Galileo! 'Mind your own business, Missy,' Felix snapped.

'Felix Frost!' Mrs Banks turned and shouted at him.

'You're a liar, Felix,' Missy snorted.

'Right, the two of you, stay behind after class,' Mrs Banks sighed.

This wasn't the first time Missy and Felix had found themselves in detention together. *It won't be the last time either.* Felix took a long, frustrated breath at the thought. *Not until Missy gets off my case once and for all.*

The end of class bell rang. As everyone else packed up their bags and headed out of the door, Missy and Felix stayed sat in their seats.

'Both of you are going to spend the next hour reading your physics textbooks,' Mrs Banks instructed, packing up her bag and shrugging on her coat. 'Chapter twelve. And I'll have five hundred words from you both about the force chain created by quicksand on my desk first thing on Monday morning.'

Felix opened up his textbook without so much as a glance in Missy's direction. He heard the door swing on its hinges as Mrs Banks left the classroom. His eyes scanned over the heading of chapter twelve: *'The Physics of Quicksand'*.

Galloping Galileo! This is all I need — I have a time machine sitting under my bed and here I am re-reading physics I learned when I was still in nappies!

Felix slammed the book shut and rubbed his temples in frustration.

'What's the matter, Felix?' Missy muttered, sounding bored. 'Used your eidetic memory to whizz through the book in a matter of seconds?'

'An eidetic memory is the ability to recall things in exact detail, not being able to read a book in a few seconds,' Felix corrected her, annoyed.

'Most normal people don't even know what eidetic means,' Missy sighed in her bored voice.

'You're not reading the textbook,' Felix pointed out. It lay untouched on the table in front of Missy.

'Don't need to.'

'Already read it?' he guessed.

She nodded. 'Unlike you, Felix, I don't come from a long line of scientific geniuses. I actually need to read my textbooks in order to do well at school.'

Felix snorted in disbelief. 'What makes you think I come from a long line of geniuses?'

'Don't you?' Missy shrugged. 'I bet your parents are both nuclear physicists or brain surgeons or something.'

'Not even close. My dad drives trains and my mum's a part-time dental nurse.'

'And I bet they're both really clever.'

'They're not,' Felix replied honestly.

'I bet you're lying.' Missy narrowed her eyes. 'You

might hang around with the school idiots, but I know you're not half as stupid as you pretend to be.'

'I'm not lying. You need to drop this whole "Felix is a genius" campaign. It's not true and it's boring.'

'Not boring to me.'

Why can't she just leave me alone!

'What about you then?' Felix asked, hoping to deflect attention away from himself. 'What do your parents do?'

'No idea about my dad. Haven't heard from him since my first birthday. My mum's a history whizz though. She's a curator of Roman archaeology at the British Museum.'

Felix's jaw fell slack and his eyes glazed over. He knew he was staring at Missy but couldn't help himself.

'What?' Missy asked, wiping her face, looking paranoid. 'Is there another one of Derek's bogies on my shoulder or something?'

'I didn't know your mother worked at the British Museum.'

'Why would you?' Missy snapped.

Missy turned her attention away from Felix

and pulled out her phone from her school blazer. As she began scrolling, Felix stared at the back of her head, deep in thought. *Missy's mum is a Roman archaeologist . . . and I've just been to Ancient Rome. I wonder what's the mathematical probability of such a coincidence . . .*

'You're staring at me again,' Missy said.

'Um . . . er . . .' Felix stuttered. 'So what kind of stuff does your mum do at the museum?'

'Well right now she's pretty preoccupied with the discovery of the gladiator.'

'The what?'

'Come on, it's been all over the news. Everyone's talking about it.'

'Not in my house they're not.' *They only talk about football.* 'What gladiator?' Missy paused for a moment before reaching into her school bag and pulling out a newspaper article. She handed it to Felix.

Felix unfolded the torn-out piece of newspaper and nearly stopped breathing when he saw what was printed on it.

Next to the article was a picture of a gladiator's

golden helmet. He recognized it straight away. Felix had been face-to-face with that helmet when he'd travelled back in time the night before.

It was the helmet of Attilius.

ROMAN MURDER MYSTERY

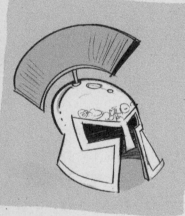

The remains of a murdered Roman man have been unearthed in an elderly woman's back garden.

Eighty-nine-year-old Ethel Davies had the shock of her life when workmen began to dig the foundations of her new conservatory, and instead dug up the remains of an ancient warrior.

'The arrowhead found embedded in the skeleton's chest leads us to believe that he died from an arrow wound to the heart,' announced Professor Debbie Six, curator of Roman artefacts at the British Museum. 'Beyond that we

know two things for certain. Firstly, this man lived a violent life. The skeleton's fractured bones are typical of injuries found in Roman gladiators. And secondly, whoever this man was, he was incredibly important.

'Two gold coins dating back to the reign of Emperor Nero were placed over the man's eyes – a typical Roman burial. But what is more remarkable is that the man was buried in full gladiatorial armour,' confirmed Professor Six. 'Body armour, a brilliant sword and shield, and a solid-gold helmet engraved with unusual markings and an image of Mars – the Roman god of war. The helmet alone is priceless, and possibly the single most amazing Roman artefact to have ever been unearthed in the UK.'

The race is now on for historians to solve this two-thousand-year-old murder mystery. Who was this Roman gladiator? Why was he so important? Why did he meet such a terrible end? Carbon dating suggests

5
Axes, Swords and Golden Coins

The newspaper cutting fell from Felix's hands and fluttered to the ground.

'Where's the helmet?' Felix demanded.

'At the museum,' Missy replied, looking confused.

'I need to see it. NOW!'

'You can't.' Missy bent down and picked up the piece of newspaper. She carefully folded it back up and put it in her pocket. 'It's not on display for the general public. And anyway, the museum closes in an hour – you'd never get there in—'

'But you must have access to the helmet,' Felix said, thinking quickly. 'Or at least your mum must.'

'Yeah, so?'

'I need to see it.'

'Why?'

'Why does it matter?' Felix screwed up his fists in frustration. 'I shouldn't have to explain myself to—'

'Actually, you should explain yourself if you want me to sneak you behind the scenes at the museum to look at one of the most important Roman artefacts ever dug up in this country.'

The words stung Felix's ears like wasp stings. *This country. What was Attilius's helmet doing in this country? Why wasn't he buried in Rome?*

'Please, Missy,' Felix started to beg. 'I need to see the helmet. I'll do anything.'

'Will you join the maths and science clubs?' Missy said quickly. 'We have a maths competition coming up – we need someone like you on the team.'

'No.' Felix shook his head. 'I'm no good at maths and science, I keep telling you . . .'

Missy spun around and started packing up her school bag. She swung the bag over her shoulder and made for the door.

'Missy, wait.' Felix jumped up and grabbed her shoulder. Missy turned around and looked at Felix's hand in disgust before shrugging away from him. 'OK, fine. I'll join your stupid clubs—'

'It's not stupid.'

It's stupid to me. I could do maths like that standing on my head with my eyes closed, while playing a samba on a tin whistle!

'I'll join your clubs, I promise. Just please, please . . . I need to see that helmet. Please.'

Missy glared at him, chewing her lip in thought. 'Meet me in the Roman section of the museum at ten o'clock tomorrow morning.'

* * *

The next morning, Felix boarded a train to London with Einstein in his pocket. No one asked him where he was off to as he left the house. *The statistical probability of them even noticing I'm not there is pretty low,* Felix told himself, as the train pulled into King's Cross Station. *They'll be glued to the TV all day — the football's on.*

From King's Cross Station it was only a short walk to the British Museum. Felix stood outside for a moment, looking up at the huge white building flanked by rows of stone columns. *Just like a Roman temple*.

Inside the museum a huge glass domed roof stretched into the sky. *Half Roman temple, half spaceship*, Felix thought with a smile.

Felix walked among hundreds of visitors bustling through the Great Court – the central hub of the museum. He watched excited children queue up in the gift shop, and hordes of tourists make their way into the Ancient Egyptian and Aztec wings to peer at ancient treasures.

Most people come to a museum to learn about the past. But I have a time machine. I could go there myself . . . but time travel is wrong. It's wrong, Felix tried to convince himself. *I can't do it again.*

Felix followed the signs to the Roman rooms. He climbed the steep museum steps, weaving his way through the crowds. Einstein poked his head out of Felix's pocket to get a better view. 'I'd keep hidden if I were you, buddy,' Felix whispered. 'I don't think pet lizards are allowed in here – even ones as intelligent as you.'

The Roman rooms were vast. One room had artefacts about Roman farming, village life, fishing, weaving and pottery. Felix glanced at the objects behind glass as he moved through the rooms. He stopped when he came to the section on Roman gladiators.

GLADIATORS

For more than 650 years, gladiatorial contests were held in the areas ruled by Rome, and thousands of men and women were killed in combat or by animals for the entertainment of the people . . .

'It doesn't say anything about children fighting to the death as entertainment,' Felix said under his breath. 'I wonder if archaeologists even know how twisted some of the Roman emperors could be?'

'I didn't think you'd show up,' said a familiar voice beside him.

Felix caught Missy's eye in the reflection of the glass cabinet in front of them.

'I promised I'd join the science club. And you promised you'd show me Attilius's helmet.'

Missy looked down at Felix's feet. 'I hope you're good at tiptoeing. We've got some serious sneaking around to do.'

Missy led Felix towards a door that said 'STAFF ONLY' above it. The door was guarded by a security man in a suit with a walkie-talkie in his hand.

'There's a tourist drawing a moustache on the marble statue of Julius Caesar,' Missy said to the guard, wide-eyed.

He frowned, muttered something into the walkie-talkie and ran off, leaving the door unattended.

After a quick glance over his shoulder, Felix followed Missy through the 'STAFF ONLY' door.

It led to a long dark corridor. Missy began to run and Felix picked up his pace too. They rushed past doors labelled 'Aztec Masks', 'African Swords', 'DO NOT ENTER' and 'KEEP OUT!'.

'Have you ever been in there?' Felix asked, pointing to a door that said 'Iron Age Tools' above it.

'Shhh!' Missy whispered, glaring at Felix over her shoulder. 'If someone catches us in here we'll be out on the street faster than you can say "flint axe". And yes,' she said, nodding. 'Of course I've been in there. I've been in every room that's out of bounds. What else am I meant to do at the weekends?'

Missy Six = class prefect and rebel. Black holes and comet tails, who would have thought that . . . ?

At the end of the corridor was a narrow spiral staircase. Missy took two steps at a time and Felix followed. 'Were you brought up by a herd of elephants or something?' Missy hissed. 'Don't make so much noise.'

They arrived at the top of the staircase, and another long corridor stretched out ahead of them. 'I told you,' Missy turned around and glared at Felix, 'we need to be—'

'It would seem the race is on,' said a voice, as a nearby door handle turned and the door began to creak open.

Missy reached for the nearest door. Felix read the sign above it: 'Mummified Cats'.

He felt Missy push him into the dark room. She quietly closed the door behind them. In the dim half-light Felix could make out the shapes of hundreds of mummified cats on floor-to-ceiling shelves. Cat bodies, cat heads, cat claws.

Missy put her index finger to her lips and gave Felix a threatening glare. 'Don't say a word,' she mouthed.

'We're colleagues, Aldini,' said a female voice

outside in the corridor. 'It shouldn't be a race. We should be working together.'

'Pah!' spat a man's voice. 'The only time I'd ever work with you is to draft your resignation letter, Six. You and I both know that only one of us can be promoted to head curator, and that whoever solves this Roman murder mystery will be the one who wins the promotion. I will solve it, I will be promoted, and once I'm running this dusty old museum one of the first things I'll do is make sure that you are . . . how can I put this . . . let go, shown the door, made surplus to requirements. There's only room for one of us in this museum, Six.'

'I don't agree,' the woman argued back. 'You can threaten me and play dirty if you want, Aldini. I don't care. All I care about is getting to the bottom of this mystery – uncovering the truth. And if you were any kind of historian then you'd feel the same.'

'Like I said, Six,' the man snarled, 'the race is on.'

Felix heard two sets of footsteps walking away.

'Was that your mum out there?' he asked Missy.

'It's none of your business, Felix,' Missy snapped

back, her eyes steely with determination as she bit down on her lip. 'You've made it very clear that you don't trust me with your secrets so why should I tell you anything? You can't trust me and I can't trust you. Come on.' She reached for the door handle. 'Let's get this over with.'

They stepped out into the corridor.

'You know, Felix,' Missy paused outside a door with a 'KEEP OUT!' sign above it, her hand hovering over the doorknob, 'I never said anything about the helmet belonging to someone called Attilius.'

Felix could only stare back at her in silence. For someone so clever, he really could make stupid mistakes sometimes. 'I asked my mum last night what that word means,' Missy continued. 'Attilius. She said that it's nothing but a legend. Roman parents used to scare their children with it.'

'A famous legend,' Felix said with a shrug, hoping to cover his tracks. 'Everyone's heard of Attilius.'

Missy shook her head. 'Only experts on Ancient Rome. There's only one surviving fragment of information about Attilius – a stone tablet with an inscription carved into the base:

"Attilius! Attilius! Blood and glory be his name. Attilius! Attilius! Smite and blow and maim. Attilius! Attilius! Slaughterer of babes. Attilius! Attilius! Golden helmet, shining blade.""

The words shook Felix to the bone. They were the very same ones he'd heard the Roman crowd chant at Nero's Games, just before he'd entered the arena to die.

'Golden helmets like this one,' Missy gestured to what lay behind the door, 'are very, very rare . . . in fact this is the only one that's ever been found. It's a strange coincidence that you should know the name of the one gladiator who had a golden helmet.'

Felix tried his hardest to give nothing away.

'Coincidences aren't that mathematically interesting, Missy.'

'Well you'd know all about maths, wouldn't you, Felix?'

Missy swung open the door and stood back so Felix could walk inside the room.

The walls of the large, dimly lit room were stained grey with time, and lined with dozens of dark wooden shelves. Each shelf was packed with hundreds of dusty objects. Vases, bowls, bronze knives, daggers, coins and leather shoes – every one of them was labelled with a white tag. There must have been over a thousand objects in there.

But Felix didn't care about what sat on the shelves around him. He didn't care how important they were or why they weren't on display in the main museum. All he could think about was what lay in the middle of the room.

Set out on a table, just as it had been found in the ground, were the skeletal remains of the greatest gladiator Rome had ever seen. And next to the skeleton sat the gladiator's armour and golden helmet.

Missy walked past Felix. She carefully picked up a small, rusted metal object from the table and held it out, flat on her palm, towards Felix. 'This is the arrowhead that killed him. He wasn't wearing the armour when he was killed – otherwise there would be signs that the arrow had penetrated it. He must have been un-armoured when he was shot, then put in the armour and the helmet to be buried. And these were placed over his eyes.' Missy put down the arrowhead and picked up two shining golden coins. 'The Romans always did this with their dead – they believed the coins would be used to pay the ferryman to take them to the afterlife.'

Felix wasn't really listening to a word Missy said. He wasn't looking at the golden coins or the arrowhead. Very slowly, he began to cross the room towards the table, never once taking his eyes from the former gladiator lying there.

He stared in utter astonishment.

The bones had been bleached by the earth over centuries. Next to the skeleton's right hand was a heavy axe, blunted by time but just as menacing as Felix remembered. Placed above the skeleton's head was the golden helmet, just as brilliant in that dusty old room as it had been nearly two thousand years ago in Nero's Arena. It was just as Felix remembered it – solid gold, two narrow eye slits, above which was engraved a man holding a sword in one hand and an axe in the other. Felix pointed at the engraving. 'Is that—'

'Mars,' Missy answered. 'The Roman god of war. And this,' she pointed to the engraving on the shield of a man holding a club in his right hand, 'is Hercules, the Roman god of bravery.'

Felix hardly blinked as he stared, open-mouthed, at the objects lying on the table. He began to weigh up the evidence, calculate the possibility of coincidence. But there was no doubt in his mind. This was no coincidence.

The helmet, shield, axe, armour and bones on this table had once belonged to the greatest gladiator Rome had ever seen. Attilius.

Felix took another step forward and gazed down at the bare bones of a warrior who had been murdered so long ago.

You spent your life slaughtering the innocent, he thought. *And then someone murdered you. But who? Why? And why here in England, why not Rome?*

'There's something else you should see . . .' Missy said softly, pulling Felix from his thoughts. 'Strange markings on the helmet.'

Felix moved closer to the table. He couldn't remember seeing anything on the helmet when he'd come face-to-face with Attilius before. *Then again, I was more concerned with the fact that I was about to die . . .*

'Here.' Missy pointed to two letters that had been scratched into the side of the golden helmet.

ℱℱ

'It's strange,' said Missy thoughtfully. 'Because in Latin the letter F is usually written with a hook on the bottom. But these letters look like they've been written in a more modern style.'

'Impossible,' Felix whispered.

He recognized the two letters immediately. The two letters he'd carved into everything he'd invented for as long as he could remember.

My signature. He took a step away from the table. *How in Newton's name did it end up there . . . ?*

6
Genius Exposed

The one thing Felix Frost hated more than incorrect equations was unanswered questions.

†Ť.

My signature. On Attilius's helmet. How? Why? I didn't carve it when I was back in Ancient Rome. So how did it get there? Oh, Copernicus!

Reason and logic — there has to be some kind of explanation . . .

❋ *x = my signature*

❋ *y = I did not put my signature on the helmet the one time I was in Ancient Rome*

※ $x + y = t$ *(truth)*

※ t = *I am going to travel back to Ancient Rome again, and this time I'm going to somehow put my signature on Attilius's helmet*

But why in Aristotle's name would I want to do that? If only Missy wasn't such a dragon in a school skirt I could ask her for help. Maybe.

Felix's brain rattled like a bag of Roman bones all the way home. As soon as he stepped inside the front door he could hear the sound of the television in the living room. The football was on, which meant that Freddie, Frank, Dad and Mum would all be sat in front of it like zombies. They didn't notice the sound of Felix closing the door behind him, climbing the stairs and opening and shutting his bedroom door – or, if they did hear, they ignored it.

Einstein crawled out of Felix's pocket and sprang through the air. He landed by the foot of Felix's bed. His front left foot rose up, pointing under the bed, and his scales flashed a deep shade of **scarlet**.

'Danger?' Felix looked at Einstein. 'What's dangerous?'

Einstein rolled his huge eyes towards the dark space beneath Felix's bed.

'How did you know what I was thinking?' Felix asked his pet lizard, shocked. Einstein rolled his eyes again. 'OK, OK. Am I that obvious? Yes, you're right – I think we should fire up the time machine again. Yes, I think we should blast back to Ancient Rome. Yes, I have decided that's the only way we'll ever know the truth about Attilius's helmet – and, who knows, maybe we'll find a way to save Lucius and all those other kids from being killed. And yes, I realize it's dangerous . . . but what choice do we have?'

Einstein threw his front legs up into the air, arching his back in frustration and rolling his eyes towards the sky. There was no colour in Einstein's ability to communicate just how stupid he thought Felix was being at that moment in time.

Felix grabbed an old backpack from beneath his bed, then pulled out the time machine. He set the first part of the time machine – the old microwave – on one side of his bedroom, and the hotplate on the other side – just how it had been when he'd used it before.

Then he moved around his room like lightning, opening drawers and pulling out bits and pieces, stuffing them into the backpack as he went. 'What will I need . . . what will I need?' he muttered frantically. 'A magnet – of course – copper wire, a block of magnesium, a torch, batteries, a potato – to use when the batteries run out, obviously – a catapult, a pen and paper, a periscope, food.' He pulled out the last of his secret crisps and biscuits stash and shoved it into the bag. 'My Roman toga. A space blanket to keep me warm at night, a ball of string – endless possibilities with that – and a magnifying glass, and . . .'

'Who are you speaking to?'

Felix spun around to see Missy standing in his bedroom doorway.

'W-what are you . . . ?' he stuttered. 'How did you . . .'

'Relax,' she said, walking into the room and plonking herself down on Felix's bed. 'The front door was wide open – I walked straight into your house. I did stick my head around the door to your living room to introduce myself to your family, but they were kind of preoccupied.'

'They get like that when the football's on,' Felix explained. 'Missy, you shouldn't be here.'

Missy didn't respond – she was too busy staring at Felix's bedroom walls in wonder. 'Did you do all of this?' She pointed at the hundreds of scientific equations scrawled across the walls. 'Felix, some of this stuff looks really advanced.'

'You don't even know what you're looking at,' Felix argued, feeling panicked. *I'm not ready for the truth to come out . . . I'm not ready . . .* 'It's not advanced maths . . . it's—'

'Felix!' Missy held her hand out to silence him. 'Enough. Don't bother lying to me. I might not understand these equations but I'm not stupid. And neither are you, so stop denying it.'

'Missy . . . for the love of evolution . . . in Newton's name . . . why are you here?' Felix demanded, flustered.

'Evolution and Newton? Yep, you're definitely joining the science club. No excuses. And don't you want to talk about this?' Missy gestured to the nearest equation on Felix's bedroom wall. 'Or this?' She pointed to the homemade microscopes, helix models and advanced textbooks sitting on his bookshelves. 'Or this?' she shrieked, staring at the time machine. 'Or the fact that I'm pretty sure I just caught you speaking to a lizard?'

Felix shouted, 'All of those things are none of your business. What are you doing here in my bedroom? Spying on me?'

'As if,' Missy snorted. 'There's something else from the museum I wanted to show you . . .' She swung her backpack from her shoulders and on to the ground, then opened it up and pulled out a clear plastic bag stuffed with rusted objects.

'Missy . . . what on earth . . . ?'

'I've "borrowed" these from the museum.' She plunged her hand into the plastic bag. 'Mum doesn't know. But I'm doing it to help her.'

Missy pulled out a handful of rusted Roman treasure.

She moved towards Felix's bed and carefully laid the items from the bag on to his bedcovers. 'A ring, a fortune's worth of golden coins – all of them from Rome during Nero's reign – what we think are a pair of glasses, and this . . .' She held up what looked like a metal buckle. The buckle was in the shape of a circle with an arrow coming out of the top right-hand corner. 'The symbol on the buckle stands for Mars – the Roman god of war. He was associated with gladiators, soldiers – anyone who fought to the death.'

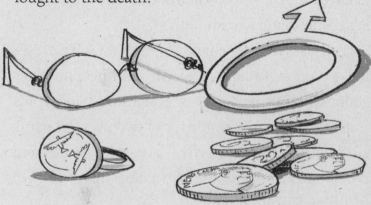

But Felix wasn't looking at the buckle. He wasn't even looking at the fortune of golden coins.

He was looking at the ring.

It had oxidized with age, bent and battered over time, but Felix recognized it instantly.

Two hawks circling one another in the sky.

Lucius's ring!

Felix picked up the ring and rolled it between his fingers. 'Missy, where did you get this from?'

'This stuff was found with the Roman skeleton, along with the helmet and the other armour. But the museum are keeping quiet about these things for now.'

Attilius must have stolen the ring after he killed Lucius, thought Felix. *A murderer and a thief!* 'Why are the museum keeping quiet?'

'Because they're clues.' Missy's big blue eyes looked up at Felix. 'All of these things are clues about who this person was. A sealstone ring, coins from Nero's Rome – not just the two over the man's eyes but a fortune's worth – a pair of glasses and a belt buckle. These are the items that will help historians identify him.'

'But isn't that what the museum want?' Felix asked, confused. 'To find out who Attilius was? How he ended up with all these things?' He looked down at Lucius's ring in his hand.

The thought of Attilius prising Lucius's ring from his cold fingers after he'd killed him made Felix's stomach churn.

'Artefacts like this have never been dug up in England before,' Missy explained, taking a deep breath. 'They're of incredible historic importance. Until we know their significance then it's best to keep quiet about them.'

'So you thought you'd steal them? Sneak into

my house and wave them around as if they were chocolate bars?'

'I told you,' Missy said, sounding offended, 'I didn't sneak into your house, the door was wide open! The truth is, Felix, I need your help. I don't know who else to ask – you're the cleverest person I know.'

'You've got me wrong.' Felix shook his head. 'I might be good at maths and science, but I don't know anything about Ancient Rome.'

'You're also good at lying.' Missy narrowed her eyes. 'And I'm good at knowing when you're lying. I know you're lying about this. You know more about Ancient Rome and Attilius than you say you do.'

Seriously, science fiction couldn't conjure up a more annoying arch-enemy than Missy Six! Why can't she just LEAVE ME ALONE!

'You heard what Professor Aldini said to my mum at the museum – if she doesn't find out who this murdered gladiator is then she'll lose her job. If she loses her job then we'll lose our house, get kicked out on the streets and starve to death!'

Missy should be in the drama club as well as science, Felix decided. *Talk about a drama queen!*

Missy bit down on her bottom lip, took a deep breath and stepped towards Felix. He instinctively took a step back. 'I'm not leaving until you at least admit to me, once and for all, that you're not as dumb as you pretend to be.'

'Why do you care?' Felix threw his hands into the air, exasperated.

'I just do.' Missy held Felix's gaze.

I'll tell you anything . . . anything to just GET YOU OUT OF MY HOUSE!

'Fine,' he sighed aloud. 'I admit it. I'm a genetic freak of nature. A thing worthy of scientific experimentation. I'm a weirdo. A nutcase. A mind-blowingly intelligent loon. I'm a boy with the brain of a computer. A—'

'A genius will do,' Missy said quietly, giving Felix the faintest of smiles.

'Now will you please leave?' Felix pointed at his bedroom door.

Missy glared at him, a look of disappointment flashing across her eyes. 'Fine,' she said through gritted teeth, putting the coins, buckle and glasses back into the clear bag. She held out her hand for the ring Felix still had. Lucius's ring. Felix reluctantly handed it over. 'I'll see you at school on Monday.' She swung her backpack on to her shoulders and stomped out of Felix's bedroom.

Felix let out a loud sigh.

'As if I didn't have enough to worry about,' Felix admitted to Einstein, who had watched the whole thing from Felix's bookcase, camouflaging himself in with the books. 'Now I have Missy on my case too?'

Einstein turned a shocking shade of **orange**. 'What are you thinking about?' Felix asked. Einstein looked towards Felix's bedroom door, where Missy had just stormed out. 'I know.' Felix realized what Einstein was trying to say to him. 'The stuff being kept a secret is a bit weird. And I don't even want to begin to think how Attilius got hold of Lucius's ring . . . I guess there's only one way we'll ever find out . . .'

Einstein pushed his way out between the books and settled beside a picture of Felix and his family, taken on their holiday to France the summer before.

The small lizard tapped his foot on the photo frame, his scales shimmering like the sun. 'My family?' Felix scratched his head. 'I'll leave them a note.'

Dear Mum, Dad, Freddie and Frank,

If you are reading this letter then it means that I am dead. Or maybe trapped in space/time vortex. I have successfully invented a time machine and have travelled back to the year 0060. Co-ordinates 56, 41 (I know you won't be able to work it out, but that's Ancient Rome).

I have taken the time machine's remote control with me so you won't be able to follow.

If all goes well, then I shall be back in a nanosecond and you won't know that I am gone.

If I don't come back then please leave the contents of my room to the Royal Scientific Society – they may be particularly interested in the contents of the mould jar by my bed.

Felix

Felix folded up the note and posted it under his bedroom door. He zipped up his backpack and put his arms through the straps. He grabbed his heavy glass safety goggles and put them on. 'Time to go time travelling . . .'

Einstein made a quick dash for the nearest hiding spot, under the bed, but Felix was too quick for him. He plucked the little lizard up by his tail. Einstein's legs scrambled in mid-air and his scales flashed shades of **red**. 'Sorry, old pal,' Felix said, putting Einstein in his pocket. 'But you're coming with me too – we're a team, remember?'

Felix picked up the old TV remote that controlled the time machine.

Then he grabbed the smoky quartz rock that had fallen into the path of the machine's laser before. He held the rock tightly in his hand, ready to throw it as soon as the laser was activated.

Felix typed in the co-ordinates for Rome into the TV remote, along with the year 0060.3 – two months before the time he'd visited before. 'That gives us more time to get to the truth,' he explained to Einstein. 'Time seemed to stand still here when we went back before. There's no reason we can't spend two months in Ancient Rome without anyone at home being any the wiser.'

Felix stood in the path of the laser beam and closed his eyes . . . His fingers hovered over the green button on the remote control.

The thudding of his own heart was enough to distract Felix from the sound of his bedroom door opening once again.

Felix brought the control up towards his chest and counted, 'One . . . two . . . three . . .'

'Felix—'

Felix's eyes shot open as he pressed down on the green button. He threw the rock into the air at the very same moment that Missy came and stood right next to him.

'Missy . . . no!'

It was too late.

A bright blue laser beam blasted out of the old microwave. It hit the tumbling rock and splintered into a thousand other tiny beams, each one hitting Felix and Missy as they stood in the line of fire.

Both Missy and Felix screamed for their lives as they felt every atom of their body rip apart and hurtle through space and time.

7
The Roman Forum

Ooomf!

Felix fell flat on his back, cobblestones digging into his spine.

'Missy!' he hollered as she landed smack bang on top of him.

'Felix!' she screamed back, pushing herself up in horror and quickly rolling off. 'What did you . . . Where . . . How . . . Why?'

'All very good questions, Missy,' Felix said, springing to his feet. 'I've got a few questions for you too – like what in Newton's name are you doing here?! But that'll have to wait. Right now I need to get you back home.' He began to fumble with the old TV remote still clutched in his hands.

'I'm not going back anywhere.' Missy snatched the remote and looked down at it, confused. 'Is this a TV remote?'

'It *was* a TV remote.' Felix snatched it back. 'It now controls my time machine.' Missy's mouth fell open. 'And I don't give a winking wormhole what you want to do – you're going back home.'

'No!' Missy grabbed the remote back again, swung her backpack off her shoulders and put the remote in it. She quickly did the bag up again and put it back on her shoulders. 'I'm staying here. And what on earth do you mean, a time mach—' Missy's voice fell away as she looked around her.

They were in the same spot Felix had arrived in before – the middle of a wide cobbled street, surrounded by large stone buildings. Only this time they had arrived in the dead of night, and the street was deserted.

Just as well, Felix quickly realized. *What was I thinking? I should have put my toga on before I left. Do I fancy finding myself on the pointy end of a Roman soldier's sword again . . . er, NO!*

'W-where . . . w-what . . .' Missy stuttered, her
eyes wide with shock and awe. 'Felix . . . what
have you done?'

There was no point in lying. ***There's no way
she'll buy the whole 'we've teleported on to a
film set' line,*** Felix decided.

'I invented a time machine,' he said simply. Missy
stared back at him blankly, as if he was speaking in
Klingon. 'I did it by accident – I was trying to invent
a teleporter.' Missy blinked rapidly, a slight frown

appearing between her eyes. 'But the machine doesn't just teleport things through space – it teleports them through time too. When I decided to use it just now, I wasn't planning on having a hitchhiker.' He scowled at Missy. 'But here you are. And here we are – in Ancient Rome.'

'Ancient . . . Ancient . . .' Missy once again looked around at the colossal stone buildings and marble statues in disbelief. 'You're lying,' she said weakly.

Felix shook his head, annoyed. 'I thought you were good at telling when I was lying? Aren't you meant to be the cleverest girl in school? Does this look like anything other than Ancient Rome to you?' He swept his arms around him in a grand gesture. 'Look, we don't have time to argue. Right now we need to disguise ourselves as Roman citizens, or before we know it we'll be caught by guards, sacrificed in a temple or fed to the lions.'

Missy looked down at the jeans and blue jumper she was wearing. 'You're right,' she muttered. 'We'll look like slaves to the Roman guards. They'll be chasing us down the street and calling out for blood if they catch sight of us . . .'

94

'That's exactly what happened to me before.' Felix rummaged around in his backpack. 'Why do you think I packed this . . .' He pulled out the red material he'd used as a toga the last time.

'You've been here before?' Missy said, her eyes bulging out of their sockets. 'You own a toga?'

'I told you – explanations can wait.' Felix looked around at their surroundings. *Missy needs a toga . . . Missy needs a toga . . . I'm not going to find another market stall to borrow from in the middle of the night . . .*

'Here.' Felix took his Swiss army knife out of his pocket and held one end of the fabric out towards Missy. 'There should be enough material for us both to wear. Hold this end and I'll cut it down the middle.'

Missy held it without question, and once Felix had finished cutting it in two she took her half and expertly draped it around her body into a toga. She frowned as Felix fumbled with his material. 'Let me do it,' Missy offered. 'I spent last summer helping Mum dress dozens of mannequins at the museum as part of their "Bring History to Life" campaign.

I never thought toga dressing was a skill I'd use again . . . And, Felix, you might want to take those off.' She pointed to his safety goggles, still over his eyes. 'They didn't have things like that in Ancient Rome.'

Felix shoved them into his backpack. 'We need to get out of here. We need to hide.'

He began to run down the street, his trainers slapping down on the cobblestones. *Why can I only hear the echo of one pair of feet? Oh, trumpeting tornadoes — Missy's not following me!*

Felix stopped and turned around, half expecting to see Missy underneath the boot of a furious centurion.

But Missy was just standing in the middle of the street. She slowly moved around on the spot, staring at the buildings and statues around her.

'Missy, psst . . .' Felix tried to whisper. 'Sightseeing can wait.'

'Don't you see where we are, Felix?' Missy made no attempt to be quiet. Felix ran back towards her, ready to drag her away into the safety of the shadows. 'This is the Roman Forum.'

'The what?' Felix said, looking around.

'Don't you recognize it from history books? Look.' She pointed to a small temple to their right. 'That's the Temple of Castor and Pollux – it's one of the oldest buildings in Rome. And there . . .' she ran towards another building, pointing excitedly, 'that's the Basilica Aemilia, one of the most beautiful buildings in the whole of Ancient Rome – it's where the entire city's business was done. And that,' she ran towards another building, 'is the Temple of Saturn, and there's the Roman Senate – we all know what happened there . . .' She looked over at Felix, who glanced back at her blankly. 'Er, hello!' She waved her hands around in the air. 'It's only where Julius Caesar was killed! But where's . . .' She spun around, searching the skyline for something. 'Where is it? The Colosseum . . . it should be over there, but it's not.'

'It hasn't been built yet,' Felix said. 'I'm not as good at history as you are, but I know that the Colosseum was built in 70 AD – that's two years after Nero died.'

'We've come back to Nero's reign?' Missy shrieked.

Felix nodded. 'Well that's just great!' Missy threw her hands up. 'You do know that Nero was the craziest, most bloodthirsty, psychotic emperor there was? I heard he had his brother fed to the lions because he didn't laugh at one of his jokes.'

'Charming.' Felix shook his head, frustrated. 'We really need to hide.'

Missy nodded. 'I know where we can go.'

She ran out of the main square, between two temples and down a dark alleyway. Felix followed her, amazed that she seemed to know the Ancient Roman streets by heart. After a few minutes they came to a crumbling temple. Felix pulled the torch he'd brought with him out of his bag. They sat down inside the damp, empty old temple, their backs pressed against the wall.

'The Romans stopped using this temple in Emperor Tiberius's reign – that was ages ago,' Missy said, catching her breath.

Jeez, she's like a walking encyclopedia! thought Felix. *She's making me feel dumb!*

Felix rummaged around in his bag and pulled out the biscuits he'd packed. He felt Einstein crawl

out of his pocket, up his arm
and settle on the packet.
'Biscuit?' Felix
offered Missy.

She looked at the
lizard sitting on the
packet in horror.

'Oh, that's just Einstein,' Felix told her. 'My
pet chameleon. I trained him to tell me what he's
thinking using the colour of his scales.'

Missy took a biscuit out of the packet and eyed
Einstein warily in the torchlight.

'I knew you were talking to a lizard before I came
into your bedroom.' A long silence fell between the
two of them, before Missy said, 'Were you ever
going to tell someone you invented a time machine?'

'No. Travelling back in time is more trouble than
it's worth. I've only done it once before and it was a
disaster.'

'What happened?'

'It's a long story.' Felix sighed. 'Basically I nearly
ended up being killed in Nero's gladiator games
in front of thousands of bloodthirsty Romans.'

He looked at Missy out of the corner of his eye. She was holding her half-eaten biscuit in front of her mouth, too captivated by Felix's story to take another bite. 'It was Attilius they wanted me to fight. He was real – *is* real – he's not just a legend made up to scare Roman kids. I recognized his helmet as soon as I saw it in the newspaper article.'

'And the other objects he was buried with?' Missy asked, nervously taking another nibble at her biscuit as she waited for Felix's answer. 'Did you recognize them? Do you know who Attilius was? Why he came to England? Why someone would want to murder him?'

Felix shook his head. 'I have no idea. I know a big fat zilch about the man behind the helmet – and how my signature is on it.'

'Your signature?'

'The FF scratched into the side of the helmet.' Einstein moved on to Felix's arm and Felix stroked his lizard thoughtfully. 'It's the same signature I put on all my inventions. It might be a coincidence . . . it might not. That's why I came back here – to check it out.'

'You think you might have invented Attilius's helmet?' Missy frowned.

'No – you can't invent gold. But maybe I had something to do with the helmet – or whoever wore it. But that's not all,' Felix admitted, looking down at Einstein sadly. 'When I was here before I met a boy – a child gladiator called Lucius.'

'You met a child gladiator?' Missy asked, shocked. 'There are myths that Nero sent children into the arena to fight. No one knows if they're actually true or not.'

'It's true.' Felix nodded. 'Nero sent a whole school of children into the arena to fight Attilius. I didn't stick around to watch but it doesn't take a genius to work out that they were all killed. The ring that Attilius was buried with . . .' Felix looked over at Missy, 'I recognized it. It belonged to Lucius. Attilius must have kept it like some kind of sicko souvenir.'

'This is amazing!' Missy's eyes shone in the darkness.

'Are you mad?' spat Felix. 'Killing kids is not amazing.'

Missy rolled her eyes. 'Not that, dummy. There's a two-thousand-year-old murder mystery that needs solving, and all the clues lead to Ancient Rome. And here we are – it's amazing.'

Solving an ancient murder mystery did have some appeal to Felix. And Missy was right, all the clues did lead to Rome:

* **The helmet, shield, axe and armour** – all belonged to Attilius, who lived in Ancient Rome.

* **The Roman coins** – all have Emperor Nero's face on them.

* **The ring** – once belonged to Lucius, and his family lived just outside of Rome.

* **The belt buckle** – the symbol of Mars, the Roman god of war.

* **The glasses** – the glasses . . .

Who knows what the glasses are about? Felix thought.

'Maybe you're right,' Felix said carefully. 'But

that doesn't change the fact that my main reason for coming back here is to find out the truth about Attilius's helmet and save Lucius.'

'Felix, you can't change history,' Missy said, concerned.

No one's ever travelled back in time before . . . who knows what's possible? Felix glared out into the darkness.

'I have so many questions . . .' Felix said quietly. 'Can I save Lucius? Should I? How did my name find its way on to Attilius's helmet? Why did Attilius have Lucius's ring? Not knowing the answers is killing me.'

'There isn't much you don't know, is there, Felix?'

'I'm starting to think the same thing about you,' Felix admitted.

'Felix?'

'Yes.'

'What exactly was your plan for coming back here?'

'I hadn't got that far,' he admitted.

'That doesn't surprise me. Lack of common sense is a likely quality in scientific geniuses. Good job you've got me here—'

'I wasn't exactly looking for a sidekick.'

'The lizard is your sidekick.' Missy pointed at Einstein who was quickly changing to bright pink. 'I'm your partner in crime. You worry about the science – I'll handle the practicalities.' She got to her feet and began to shake dust from her makeshift toga.

Felix stood up too. 'What do you think we should do?'

'We need to pick our way through the clues I have in my backpack. Let's start with the one we know the most about. The ring – you said you knew the person who owned it.'

'Lucius?'

Missy nodded. 'We need to start with him. What do you know about him?'

'I know he went to gladiator school.'

A mischievous smile crept on to Missy's face. 'Perfect. I bet I know just which school that was . . . Let's go.'

'To gladiator school?' Felix asked. 'Why?'

'Isn't it obvious, Felix?' Missy said over her shoulder, heading for the temple door. 'We're going to enrol!'

8
Warrior School

'How did you know this place was here?' Felix whispered in astonishment as they stood outside the school gates.

'The Mars Academy,' Missy said, glassy-eyed. 'It was the most famous gladiator school in Ancient Rome. Mum used to tell me bedtime stories about this place when I was little.'

Bedtime stories? thought Felix. *I had physics textbooks to tuck me up at night . . .*

The gates to the school were made of wrought iron. Torches burned either side of them, illuminating the collection of buildings beyond. It looked just as big as their school back home. There were a few small buildings made from wood and straw, and one large stone building in the centre of the front courtyard. There were two Latin words inscribed at the top of the stone building, above the main door.

FORTIS SCHOLAM

'Warrior school,' Missy translated.

'Yeah, I should have mentioned, something funny happens to our brains when we time travel,' Felix explained. 'Somehow the neural pathways rewire so we can understand the local language. A convenient glitch in the science – I haven't quite worked out why yet—'

'I already understand Latin, numbskull.' Missy rolled her eyes. 'Mum taught me how to read it before I even started school.'

'You there!' boomed a deep voice from the shadows beyond the gate.

Felix and Missy hadn't noticed the heavyset guard who'd spotted them standing outside the school.

'You ragamuffins!' The guard held a flaming torch above his head so he could get a better look. 'You gutter trash! Get out of here or you'll soon find yourself on the other side of these gates!'

'We want to join the school,' Missy replied quickly.

'The students in this school are slaves, child, you know that . . .' The man sounded unsure.

'But we want to be gladiators,' Missy said. 'We've run away from our families and come to Rome so we can enrol with the greatest gladiator school the history books will ever speak of. You usually have to buy slave children – but we're here for free.'

Felix glanced sideways at Missy in horror. *Begging to enrol in a gladiator school for slave children . . . flying Fibonacci! That's the last time I let Missy come up with a plan!*

The man walked right up to the gates. His fat face was covered with smallpox scars, his teeth had rotted away into small black stumps and his hair had been shorn close to his scalp. 'You can't afford it,' the guard snarled.

'Push me through a wormhole and call me Andromeda!' Felix exclaimed. 'Why would anyone pay to come here? I bet half the kids don't live to see their nineteenth birthday!'

'This school trains warriors,' the guard spat back. 'Fierce, brutal, merciless warriors. Warriors who fight for glory and freedom. Warriors who will go down in the history books.'

'That's what we want.' Missy stamped down hard on Felix's foot to stop him arguing.

Black holes and comet tails! He doubled up in pain.

'We have money,' Missy said. 'How does a gold coin for the two of us sound?'

The guard's eyes widened and he licked his lips greedily. 'Three gold coins.'

'Two,' Missy shot back.

'Done.' He spat on his chubby hand and extended it through the iron bars. Felix watched in disgust as Missy spat into her palm and clapped hands with the guard.

'Done,' Missy replied.

The gates swung open with a loud groan.

Silently, the guard led Felix and Missy through the empty school courtyard towards a small wooden building on the far right. At the door he turned around, his palm flat open towards them. 'Cough up,' he demanded.

Felix watched, irritated, as Missy pulled off her backpack and turned so the guard couldn't see her reach into it. The guard frowned at the sight of the strange bag, but was too concerned about his payment to say anything. Missy reached into the bag and pulled out two of the gold coins that had been buried with Attilius.

'Missy,' Felix whispered through gritted teeth. 'Those coins belong to the museum. And now I think of it, we need to talk about the things in your backpack. Those objects belong two thousand years into the future. There are already versions of those objects here – it presents a time paradox that—'

'Felix, this guard is probably a retired killer,' Missy hissed back, handing the two coins to the guard. 'Do you really want to argue about this now?'

The guard turned the coins over in his palm, inspecting them closely before nodding. He pushed open the door to the wooden hut.

Felix and Missy peered inside.

It's a dormitory, Felix realized.

Rows of straw mattresses lined the floor, each with a snoring child asleep on it.

They felt themselves being pushed into the room. 'Lessons start at sunrise tomorrow,' the guard said before slamming the door behind them.

The room was pretty dark, but a few torches burned away on the walls, offering some light to see by. Missy pointed to the far end of the dormitory, where two empty mattresses lay unclaimed at the

110

end of the rows of sleeping children. Felix followed her through the dorm, tiptoeing past the others as they slept.

Felix looked down at the sleeping bodies. Each child wore a simple sack-like garment, and next to their straw mattress each had a wooden sword and shield. They'd written their names on their shields in red paint: 'Domitius', 'Octavia', 'Cassius', 'Livia' . . .

'New blood,' came a small voice from the end of the room.

'Lucius!' Felix recognized the small blond boy straight-away. He ran the last few steps towards him.

'How do you know my name?' Lucius sat up in bed, rubbed his sleepy eyes and squinted at Felix.

Nice one, Felix, he mentally scolded himself. *Why don't you just shout a little louder that you're a time traveller!*

'Er . . . I saw it on your shield,' Felix replied, thinking quickly and pointing down to Lucius's wooden shield by the side of his bed. It looked an awful lot more battered than any of the others.

'I'm Felix, and this is Missy.'

'Hi,' Missy said, sitting down on the empty mattress opposite Lucius.

'Pleasure to meet you both.' Lucius smiled. 'Actually . . .' The smile fell from his face. 'Nothing in this place is ever a pleasure – we are all here as slaves, after all. Did your families sell you to the school like mine did?'

'Not exactly.' Missy plonked her heavy bag down next to her straw mattress. 'But the important thing is that we're here, and we're ready to fight!'

'Calm down, gladiator girl.' Felix glowered at Missy. 'Look where we are! Shouldn't we be just a little bit freaked out right now?'

'Freaked out?' Missy shook her head and smiled. 'Are you kidding me? I've dreamed about this moment my whole life! When I was a kid I used to dress up as a gladiator and pretend to fight the cat. I used to call myself Killius Missius and I'd sleep with a wooden sword next to my bed – just like all these kids in here.'

Is Missy a few atoms short of a particle?!

'Your friend's really strange,' Lucius muttered to Felix.

'She's not my friend,' Felix said quickly. 'She's my unlikely travelling companion.'

'Whatever.' Missy rolled her eyes. 'I'm getting some shut-eye before sunrise. If what I've heard is correct we'll be fighting each other from dawn until dusk.' Missy picked up her backpack and laid it under her head to use as a pillow, before closing her eyes.

'How long have you been here?' Felix asked Lucius, lying down on the empty bed next to him and taking his own bag off his back to use as a pillow.

'A whole year,' Lucius replied woefully. 'And I'm the worst in the class, so if I were you I'd probably want to hang around with one of the other boys. Domitius and Cassius – they're the boys you'd want to—'

'Hey!' Felix said, feeling cross. 'I bet you're a really

good fighter. You just haven't honed your skills yet. I bet one day you'll be the greatest warrior Rome has ever seen. Even greater than Attilius.'

'No one's greater than Attilius,' Lucius said, resting his head on his pillow and staring over at Felix.

'We'll see about that.' Felix winked at him. 'But Missy's right,' he admitted reluctantly. 'We should get some rest.'

Lucius nodded. 'We have net fighting first thing in the morning. The last time I had that class I got my feet caught in the net, fell flat on my face and everyone laughed at me. It was awful – I was so tangled up Domitius poked me with his sword until I was blue with bruises. I would have been as dead as Pluto if that had been a real fight.'

'Don't worry, Lucius.' Felix felt his eyes getting very heavy as he let out a yawn. 'We're here to help you now. "As dead as Pluto."' Felix smiled to himself. 'Why would you be as dead as a large rock that's not even classed as a planet any more?'

'A planet? Pluto's the god of the underworld,' Felix heard Lucius reply as he drifted off to sleep. 'Every Roman child knows that . . .'

9
Retiarius

Felix woke up to his nose hair being yanked. 'Good morning, Einstein.' Felix prised one eye open. 'So I wasn't dreaming,' he yawned. 'We're back in Ancient Rome again.' Felix sat up in bed and stretched, watching the other children pick up their wooden swords and shields and head outside for their first training session of the day.

Einstein scrambled over Felix's face, down his neck and then sat on his shoulder. The lizard reached up and grabbed Felix's ear to pull his head left. 'Ouch!' Felix protested, before noticing what Einstein wanted to show him.

At the foot of his bed were a brown tunic and a set of leather sandals.

Missy was already putting on the tunic and sandals that had been left out for her.

'You should put yours on too.' Felix turned around to see Lucius standing staring at him. 'You can't fight in . . .' he looked between Missy and Felix curiously, 'whatever it is you're both wearing.'

The tunics were made of a coarse, sack-like material. 'This itches like mad!' Missy complained, pulling it over her head. As Lucius bent down to pick up his sword and shield Missy whispered to Felix, 'Use your toga material to hide your clothes and rucksack. We don't want people asking questions.'

Felix yawned again and nodded. 'Good idea. Sorry, buddy.' Felix carefully put Einstein on his straw mattress. 'There's no room for you underneath these clothes. Besides, it's probably safer if you stay here. And you can keep watch – if anyone comes sniffing around our bags, come and let me know.'

'I'm starving,' Missy said to Lucius, as they followed him out of the dormitory and into the vast school courtyard. 'What's for breakfast?'

'Breakfast?' Lucius laughed. 'What do you think

this place is? Nero's court? We're lucky if we get to eat before dinnertime.'

'Everyone knows that you need energy to fight,' Felix complained. Missy shoved him hard in the ribs. 'Ouch! The science of needing food as fuel is hardly cutting edge, Missy,' he whispered, one hand on his growling stomach. 'I'm not giving anything away . . .'

'We get our meals after we've earned them,' Lucius told him. 'And to earn them you need to—'

'Smash your opponent's head in with an axe!' Missy said cheerfully.

Felix pulled on Missy's tunic, holding her back from the rest of the crowd. 'Missy, don't forget why we're here.'

'Felix,' Missy said seriously. 'I'm guessing you've spent every moment of your spare time writing scientific equations on your bedroom walls, trying to unravel the mysteries of the universe—'

'The workings of your brain are the biggest mystery of all!'

Missy folded her arms over her chest. 'Science is your thing, and this is mine. I've always dreamed about coming back to Ancient Rome, and being a gladiator. And yes, I know we have a job to do here, and I know that if we don't get home in one piece in time for dinner then I'll be grounded for the next two thousand years, but right now all I care about is picking up that net and learning how to fight.'

Felix shook his head. *Missy could argue her way out of a black hole if she tried—*

OOMF!

Someone slammed a wooden shield into Felix's stomach. 'For you, new blood.' A tall, stocky, spotty teenager loomed over him. The boy threw another shield at Missy and held his own shield out in front of him.

'Domitius,' Felix read the name on the shield.

'Yeah,' growled Domitius. 'That's my name, pipsqueak – don't forget it! It's going down in the history books. I'm the best fighter in this school – one day I'll be the best gladiator in Rome.'

'I've read a lot of history books,' Missy whispered to Felix, as Domitius waddled off. 'I've never heard of a gladiator called Domitius.'

Domitius walked over to speak to a large guard,

who Felix assumed was the instructor. Felix noticed something about the boy that was different from all of the other children in the courtyard. His scratchy brown tunic was cinched in at the waist with a leather belt, and in the middle of the belt was a shining brass belt buckle – in the shape of a circle with an arrow pointing out of the top right-hand corner.

'Recognize that?' Missy nudged Felix. She'd noticed the buckle too.

'A belt buckle with the symbol of Mars on it,' Felix said. 'Just like the one buried with Attilius. Why is Domitius wearing it?'

'You two!' shouted the instructor, pointing at Missy and Felix. 'Get your battleaxe-brandishing backsides over here and grab a net.'

'My pleasure.' Missy smiled as she ran off towards the crowd of children in the middle of the courtyard.

There were two training nets left on the ground – one for Felix and one for Missy. They looked a bit like old-fashioned fishing nets – nothing special, and certainly not something you might use to kill someone with.

Felix scooped his net off the ground and studied it suspiciously. *I've seen spiderwebs in my bedroom that look stronger . . .* His gaze rose to study the instructor standing at the centre of the crowd. The man was the tallest person Felix had ever seen.

'To be a winning retiarius,' the instructor shouted, interrupting Felix's thoughts, 'you need to use your net as though it were an extension of your arm.'

'Retiarius?' Felix whispered to Missy.

'That's what they call gladiators who fight with nets,' she whispered back.

'Is that what Attilius is?'

'No, he fights with a sword and a shield and

wears a huge helmet. He's a murmillo. Felix, don't you know anything?'

I know that the speed of light travels at 186,000 miles per second. I know that DNA was discovered in 1869. I know that the universe contains over a hundred billion galaxies . . .

'Pair up!' the instructor yelled. 'Only nets and shields allowed.'

'Is that it?' Missy turned to Felix, disappointed. 'What about battle tactics? Training exercises? How are we expected to learn anything?'

'Looks like Lucius already has a partner,' Felix pointed out. Domitius had paired up with Lucius and was already laughing at him tangled up in a net, flapping around like some kind of dying fish. 'No wonder Domitius thinks he's the best student here if the only person he ever fights is—'

Before Felix could finish he found himself flat on his back on the ground. Missy stood over him triumphantly, net in hand. 'Get up, Felix – fight back!'

Felix pushed himself to his feet and made a vague attempt to block Missy's next net whip.

'You saw Domitius's buckle?' Missy said as she flicked her net at Felix again. He quickly raised his shield to cover his face, the net making a loud whipping noise as she landed each blow.

'Not so hard, Missy, we're only practising, remember? I've never done this before! And yes, I saw Domitius's buckle – what do you think it means?'

'I think it means that Attilius took the belt buckle from Domitius after he killed him—'

CRACK! Another blow landed on Felix's shield.

'Just like he stole Lucius's ring—'

WHIP!

'As if killing people wasn't bad enough—'

CRASH!

'Attilius then stole from their dead bodies—'

The next time Missy's net came flying through the air towards Felix, he ducked down and used his own net to whip at her feet. The motion knocked her to the ground.

'Good work, Felix.' Missy smiled as she got back on her feet. 'See, I told you this would be fun . . .'

I'd rather time travel right into the path of a hungry T-rex, thought Felix.

The class spent the rest of the morning perfecting their net skills. Felix quickly learned that there were several different and effective ways to use your net in order to fight:

※ *Flick the net out in a whipping motion to knock your opponent off their feet.*

※ *Whip your opponent with the net.*

※ *Throw it over your opponent's head and tangle them up in knots.*

By the time Felix and Missy were getting the hang of retiarius fighting, the sun blazed high above them and they felt weak with hunger.

'Time for food!' came the instructor's voice.

'At last!' Felix threw down his net. 'Look at the sun. It must be at least midday by now – we've been doing this all morning!'

As Felix and Missy joined the end of the long queue snaking into the main stone building, Lucius ran up beside them. 'You two were really good,' he said, impressed.

No, you were just really, really bad, thought Felix.

'Is every training session like that?' Felix said aloud, feeling utterly exhausted.

Lucius shrugged. 'Some days we fight with spears. Sometimes axes, swords and shields. Other days we do nothing but run around the courtyard in circles. Pointless.'

'Not pointless.' Missy barged past the two boys, her nose twitching at the scent of food. 'You need to run fast in order to fight in the arena. How can you learn to run fast unless you practise?'

The queue led them into a vast hall filled with wooden tables where everyone was sitting down to eat. Missy made a beeline for the food.

'At least this afternoon's practice should be better,' Felix said to Lucius. 'Everything's always easier on a full stomach.'

'This afternoon's practice?' Lucius picked up a wooden bowl from a large pile on the ground and blew out the dirt from it. He held it up to the guard dishing out food. 'We only have one practice a day.'

'What?' asked Felix, startled. He picked up a wooden bowl and held it out to the guard. 'What are we doing this afternoon then?'

'Sewing up holes in socks. Brushing the guards' boots. Shining the school gates – things like that.'

'How are we ever meant to improve as fighters if we only have a few hours a day to practise – and on an empty stomach?'

'I don't need to improve.' Lucius led Felix to Missy already sat at the end of a wooden table, hungrily eating the food in her bowl. 'One day soon my parents will come and buy my freedom – all these lessons are pointless.'

'But what if your parents don't come and buy you out of here?' Felix tried to sound as kind as he could. 'I don't mean they don't want to,' he added quickly. 'Of course they must. But what if they can't afford to?'

'It'll be years before I'm old enough to fight in the arena. We don't graduate from school until we're at least eighteen. There's loads of time for my parents to save up enough money to buy me back,' he said confidently.

If only he knew . . .

Felix sat down, took one look at his food and nearly hurled.

What in Newton's name is that . . . ? Some kind of cold meat . . . Looks like chicken, smells like dog . . .

He tentatively put a small scrap of meat on his tongue, then spat it straight back out.

'It tastes like that time I accidentally ate a spider! What is this?'

'Stuffed dormouse,' Lucius replied, the tiny leg of the creature he was munching hanging out of the corner of his mouth.

'Isn't that meant to be a delicacy here in Rome?' Felix asked sceptically.

'This is not a mouse.' Missy prodded her plate.

'No,' Lucius agreed. 'It's probably a rat fished out of the gutter . . . but if you close your eyes and imagine the taste of vine leaves and spices you can just about pretend it's a dormouse.'

Felix dry-retched into his mouth and reached for the nearest goblet of water.

'If you're going to be sick then go outside,' Lucius said, licking his fingers before pointing to a side door in the vast hall. 'If the guards see you puke in here you'll be whipped.'

'Does the school have its own vomitarium?' Missy asked.

Felix didn't stick around to hear the answer. He headed for the side door. *Please don't be a vomitarium . . . I really need to just get some fresh air . . .*

He walked through the door.

Phew, not a vomitarium.

Felix had walked into a small room with a few wooden stalls and what looked like an Ancient Roman noticeboard on the far wall.

Felix walked towards the noticeboard, taking deep breaths and trying to forget the smell of baked rat. His eyes scanned the notices, all of which were written in Latin, and all of which he understood.

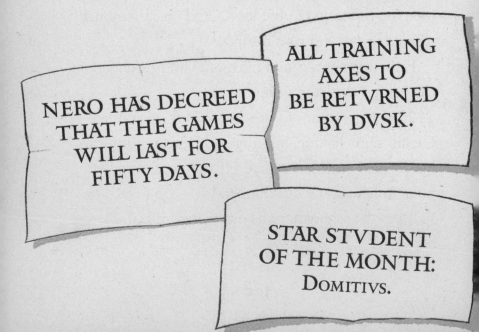

ALL TRAINING AXES TO BE RETVRNED BY DVSK.

NERO HAS DECREED THAT THE GAMES WILL LAST FOR FIFTY DAYS.

STAR STVDENT OF THE MONTH: DOMITIVS.

Among them was a poster, the word 'ATTILIUS' at the top drawing Felix's attention.

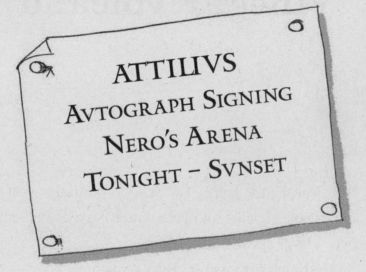

Felix stepped back from the poster with only one thought in his head: **We have to be there . . .**

10
Vinegar Volcano

'You can't just leave the school grounds, that's impossible,' Lucius told Felix and Missy, as he bent over a large spearhead.

'Nothing's impossible,' Felix replied.

Every student in the school was sitting inside the large courtyard in front of the main school building. After the sorry excuse for lunch, everyone had been put to work cleaning spearheads, swords and axes for the Roman army.

Before they'd started, Felix had had time to dart back into the dormitory to collect Einstein. 'Practice is over for the day, little guy,' he'd reassured him. 'You can hang out with us now.'

'Now *this* is a proper sword!' Missy held up a

sharp blade, its edges glinting in the sunlight. 'Why can't we train with weapons like this?'

'They belong to the centurions,' Lucius told them. 'These sword edges have seen more blood than the temple of Diana on a full moon.'

'Temple of Diana?' Felix raised his eyebrow.

Missy kicked Felix hard under the table. 'The Roman goddess of hunting, Felix, you know that . . .'

'Everyone knows that.' Lucius eyed him suspiciously.

What in the name of evolution is wrong with me? Lucius is right, every Roman child would know that!

'We need to find a way to get to Nero's Arena tonight,' Felix tried to deflect the attention back on to the important matter of Attilius's autograph signing.

'I told you,' Lucius said. 'We're not allowed out of the school gates.'

'You must all sneak out sometimes?' Missy asked, examining the sharpness of the blade she polished.

Lucius shook his head. 'The school have a policy that if anyone runs away then another student is locked in the ditch for a month.'

'The ditch?' Missy asked.

'It's a hole in the ground where there's only enough room to stand up. And you have nothing but worms to eat.'

Can't be worse than stuffed rat, thought Felix.

'So if we sneak out, then we have to sneak back in before anyone notices we're gone,' Felix said with certainty. 'We can't be responsible for anyone being locked in the ditch – not even someone like Domitius.'

'Why is it so important to go to the autograph signing anyway?'

'It's important that we get a good look at Attilius,' Felix said quickly, before Missy had a chance to reply. 'If you're going to come face-to-face with this guy in the arena then we need to know every little thing about him. Does he sign autographs with his left or right hand? Because I'd bet a year's subscription to *New Scientist Magazine* that it's the same hand he holds a sword in. It's important to know everything about your opponent before you face them. Even football teams watch the other team before they play each other. OUCH!' Felix reached down to his shin – where Missy had once again kicked him – and rubbed it.

'What's a football team?' Lucius asked, confused. 'And why would I have to fight Attilius? I won't graduate from this place until I'm eighteen – Attilius will have won his freedom long before then.'

Felix felt Einstein dig his claws in beneath his tunic. He knew he'd be glowing **red** with danger after hearing what Felix had just blurted out.

Oh, for the love of all things atomic, I really should just let Missy do all the talking . . .

'It's probably best that you don't ever take a word Felix says seriously,' Missy said.

Felix shook his head in agreement.

'Although he was serious about needing to get to that autograph signing tonight – can you think of a way we can sneak out of here?'

Lucius mumbled something about the guards never having their backs turned, but Felix was paying more attention to the white powder they were using to clean the swords. He rubbed it between his fingers and thought, *This looks like . . .* He sniffed the powder. *Natron. A naturally occurring form of baking soda. Used in ancient medicine, cooking and cleaning . . . interesting. That gives me an idea . . .*

'Where can I get some vinegar?' Felix blurted out.

Lucius frowned and looked at Missy. 'Is this one of the things I should ignore?'

'I've got a plan to create a diversion so we can sneak out.'

Missy studied Felix for a moment – he had a dangerous twinkle in his eye.

'How about in the kitchens?' Missy suggested.

Lucius scratched the side of his head. 'We won't be able to sneak into the kitchens. But we should be able to get into the doctor's hut. I remember last month when Domitius pushed me over in sword practice and I cut my leg. I had to have it washed out with vinegar and then sacrifice a chicken to the gods. I don't think they were listening though – the cut stung for weeks.'

'You know where the doctor's hut is?' Felix asked.

'Of course I do. I've been there more times than I've had hot dinners at this school.

In the last six months alone I've broken my arm, my big toe, two fingers and—'

'Take me there,' Felix said to Lucius. 'Missy, you collect as much of this stuff,' he pointed to the white powder, 'as you can. Meet us back here in ten minutes.'

'OK.' She nodded.

'Guard!' Felix's hand shot into the air. The guard – the same fat man who had let them into the school the night before – stomped up to him and nodded. 'Lucius needs to show me where the nearest toilet is. The baked rat really didn't agree with me – it's going to get messy if I don't get to a toilet soon.'

The guard pulled a disgusted face. 'Be back in ten minutes or your friend here,' he pointed at Missy, 'is going in the ditch.'

Felix stood up and gave Missy a reassuring nod.

Lucius led Felix away to the far side of the courtyard, and then along the side of the main school building. They were soon out of sight of the guard and the other children. 'It's behind here.' Lucius pointed towards the back of the main building. They ran as quietly as they could over the dusty ground.

There stood a single wooden hut, smoke rising from a makeshift chimney.

They could hear snoring coming from inside, and thick, sweet-smelling smoke poured out of the cracks beneath the door.

Felix carefully opened the door a smidge and peered through the gap.

He turned and said to Lucius, 'OK, don't freak out, but I have a pet lizard.' Felix took Einstein out from beneath his tunic. Lucius frowned. 'He can help us. Einstein,' he said to the lizard, lowering him to the floor. 'Sneak inside and let us know if the coast is clear.'

Einstein flashed **purple** for yes before quickly waddling off into the darkness of the little hut.

'You really are crazy.' Lucius shook his head.

A moment later Einstein poked his head out again. He was glowing bright **purple**.

'That means it's safe for us to go in,' Felix translated. Einstein quickly shimmered **orange**. 'But we need to be careful,' Felix added.

Inside the hut the room was filled with thick, sickly smoke – so dense it took Felix a few seconds to see anything. The walls were lined with rickety old wooden shelves, all crammed full with various dubious-looking pieces of Roman medical equipment. There were rusty saws, chisels and knives. Dirty bandages, metal hooks and bone drills. Next to the operating table was a selection of chewed twigs.

'I had to chomp down on one of those when the doctor poured vinegar into my wound.' Lucius shuddered at the painful memory.

In the corner of the room was a fat bald man, snoring heavily with a spilled bottle of Roman wine beside him. A large wolf-like dog slept at his feet, also snoozing loudly.

'Where's the vinegar?' Felix whispered.

Lucius pointed to a large clay jug on a nearby shelf.

Holding his breath, Felix crept into the room. The rickety wooden floorboards creaked under his weight. *Let's get this over with*, he told himself, picking up his pace and heading straight for the jug of vinegar.

The smoke wafted up Felix's nose and tickled the inside of his nostrils. He felt his nose twitch, and fought the urge to sneeze as his fingers closed around the handle of the clay jug. He gently lifted it off of the shelf, but the tickling in his nose was hard to ignore.

Whatever you do, Felix, don't . . .

'ACHOO!'

One eye of the sleeping dog shot open. It let out a deep growl from the back of its throat.

Felix looked over at the sleeping doctor. He was still fast asleep. Felix met the dog's gaze in defiance.

The dog growled again, louder this time. Felix took one step back, then another.

The dog's growl was now a bark.

'Grruff! Grruff!'

The fat man stirred in his sleep.

Felix didn't stick around to see if he woke up. He spun around and nearly crashed into Lucius before pushing him out of the hut and slamming the door behind them. 'Run!'

Felix and Lucius sprinted away, retracing their path, and arrived back at the main courtyard.

Missy glanced over her shoulder – the guard was looking the other way. She beckoned Felix and Lucius back to the table. 'Look, I have loads of the white stuff . . .'

'OK,' said Felix, putting the jug of vinegar on to the table. 'On the count of three, put every last grain of powder into this jug. It'll create a distraction and give us enough time to slip away. Ready?'

'What will the powder do?' Lucius asked, suddenly looking worried.

Felix smiled. 'Make a vinegar volcano.'

Vinegar Volcano
❋ *Baking soda + vinegar = carbonic acid*
❋ *Carbonic acid = HUGE eruption!*

'One . . . two . . . three . . .'

Missy threw a handful of powder into the vinegar jug, and right away a huge tower of white foam erupted from the top.

'Duck!' Missy shouted at the two boys.

The three friends fell to their knees and crawled underneath the tables, towards the gates. No one noticed them escape – they were too busy screaming, laughing, pointing and clapping at the enormous mess that was being made everywhere.

'Clean this up!' they heard the guard scream to the nearest child.

'Run to the gate!' Felix shouted at Missy and Lucius.

The vinegar volcano had done its job. No one saw them run through the courtyard and climb the wrought iron gates.

A huge grin spread over Felix's face as they ran through the busy Roman streets, leaving the school behind them.

Science, he thought happily. *It never fails . . .*

11
Cornered

There must have been over a thousand people queuing down the street by the time they arrived outside Nero's Arena.

'We're right at the back!' complained Lucius, as the guards jostled them to the end of the line.

'This is good,' Felix assured them. 'If we're the last people to meet Attilius then we might get more time with him.'

They stood in the boiling afternoon sun for hours.

Every few minutes they shuffled forward, gradually getting closer to the front of the queue. As the minutes ticked by Attilius fans strode past the other way, proudly inspecting their pieces of signed parchment.

Keep your head down, Felix told himself. *Don't look anyone in the eye. Don't do anything to attract attention. You're here for two main reasons, don't forget that . . .*

❊ *To see if FF has already been scratched into Attilius's helmet.*

❊ *To look for any other clues as to who Attilius is.*

'I can see him!' Lucius gasped.

There were probably fifty people ahead of them by the time they had a good view of Attilius. He sat on a wooden chair in full gladiatorial armour. On his head he wore his magnificent gold helmet.

'He must be baking hot in that helmet.' Missy shook her head in astonishment. 'You'd think he'd want to take it off when he wasn't fighting.'

'I don't think anyone's ever seen Attilius without his helmet,' Lucius remarked.

One by one, Attilius's fans approached him. The guards passed them a piece of blank parchment, which they then handed to Attilius. He dipped the end of his quill into a pot of ink before

scribbling a few letters on to it. Not only
did Attilius not speak to a single fan,
he also didn't look
up at them.

'Those two guards either side of him,' Felix said
as they got closer. 'They're more like prison guards
than bodyguards.'

'Attilius is basically a prisoner,' Missy replied.
'He's not free, remember . . . freedom is what he
fights for every time he steps into the arena – every
time he kills someone.'

They were now almost at the front of the queue,
and as Felix stood only a few steps away from
Attilius, it was like seeing him for what he really was
for the first time. Yes, he was a champion gladiator,
fearless and brutal and unbeaten in combat.

But he was also a prisoner, a slave who had to kill for others' amusement. Any fight could be his last, and his popularity was only as great as his last kill.

I actually feel kind of sorry for Attilius, Felix thought.

'There's no doubt about it, Felix,' Missy whispered in amazement. 'That's the helmet in the museum – the one that was dug up in the old lady's garden.'

'I can't see my initials on the helmet,' Felix whispered back.

'There's nothing there.' Missy shook her head. 'Not yet anyway—'

'Next!' the guard shouted at Lucius. Lucius took a few shaking steps forward, and the guard shoved a filthy scrap of parchment at him.

'Attilius,' Lucius whispered in awe as he approached the gladiator and held the parchment out. Attilius took the parchment without a word or a glance in Lucius's direction. 'I want you to know that I'm your biggest—'

'Next!' the guard screamed again, pushing Lucius out of the way as soon as Attilius handed the signed piece of parchment back to him.

Missy approached next. 'That helmet really is incredible,' she said to Attilius. He ignored her, snatching her piece of parchment and scribbling away. 'Where did you get it—?'

'Next!' the guard called, pushing Missy out of the way. 'This is the last boy of the day.' He looked at Felix.

'Attilius,' Felix said, standing in front of the brutish gladiator. 'You don't have to kill to win, you know that, don't you?'

Reaching for Felix's parchment, Attilius's hand paused in mid-air. Slowly, his golden helmet tilted upward as he lifted his head, and his eyes met Felix's gaze through a narrow slit.

Felix stared into Attilius's eyes. These weren't the eyes of a killer. They were filled with sadness and regret.

'You don't have to kill,' Felix repeated.

Attilius snatched the parchment from Felix and hung his head down as he signed it. 'You don't know anything, boy,' he said in a soft voice.

'That's enough!' shouted the guard, pushing Felix away.

Attilius got to his feet and the guard prodded him in the hip with a spear. Felix watched as the guards led Attilius through a set of gates and out of sight.

'Well that was no good!' Lucius exclaimed.

'We need to follow him. Einstein, climb on to the top of the gate, and let me know when the coast is clear.'

Einstein did as he was told.

He leaped on to the solid wooden gate and climbed up until he was sitting on the top. His scales turned a deep shade of **red**, which slowly began to fade to a shimmering **purple**.

'Let's go!' Felix shouted.

Felix knelt down and Missy stood on his knees, reaching for the top of the gate. She hauled herself up, and then leaned down for Lucius. After Lucius was over the gate Felix reached up and Missy pulled him on to the top of the gate. They jumped down to the ground on the other side, Einstein following and perching on Felix's shoulder.

Awesome teamwork!

They were standing inside a small courtyard. Ahead of them was a large wooden building, smoke billowing out of the top. To their left was a dark alleyway, and to their right was a collection of small wooden huts.

'Down there!' Missy pointed down the alleyway. 'I saw a glint of golden helmet.'

They ran out of the courtyard and down the alleyway. It curved to the right and came out into another courtyard. The floor was decorated with mosaics and a small fountain sat in the middle. Through a window on the far side they could see an Attilius-sized man taking off his armour.

Without a word they darted across the courtyard.

Felix led them through a door, and they found themselves in a room full of weapons – spears, nets, swords, axes and armour.

Alone, at the back of the room, stood Attilius.

He was reaching for his helmet, beginning to lift it off his head.

Attilius didn't hear the three children creep up behind him, and they didn't dare breathe as they watched him slowly lift off the golden helmet.

A long plait of golden hair fell out of the helmet.

Lucius let out a small gasp.

The slight noise was enough to catch Attilius's attention. He turned around and caught the three children standing there, staring at him.

Felix, Missy and Lucius stared back in astonishment. Einstein glowed a shocking shade of pink in disbelief before quickly camouflaging himself against Felix's tunic.

Winking wormholes!

Attilius's golden hair framed a pretty, soft face. The blue eyes that Felix had stared into only minutes before studied the three of them warily.

The secret was out.

'Y-you're a . . .' Felix stuttered, taking a step forward.

'You're a woman!'

12
The Gladiatrix

I'm Felix Frost! I detected the Higgs boson particle in my bedroom when I was ten years old. How did I not see this?

'A gladiatrix,' Missy whispered in awe.

'Who are you? Why are you here? How did you get in?' the woman said, panicking. 'Tell anyone what you've seen and I'll feed you to the lions!'

'Why were you in Attilius's armour?' Lucius asked. 'Is Attilius too busy training to sign parchments for fans, so you have to pretend to be him?'

'I am Attilius,' the woman growled. 'I'm fed up of lying. Well, my name's Attilia, to be exact . . . but no one's called me that for years.'

'Who knows you're a woman?' Felix asked.

'Nero, a few of the guards . . . no one else. I'm careful that no one sees me without my armour or helmet on.'

'Hang on a minute . . .' Missy shook her head in confusion. 'You're telling us that you are, and always have been, Attilius. The greatest gladiator that ever lived. The longest-reigning champion in history, the most feared, revered, celebrated and decorated gladiator Rome has ever seen.'

Attilia nodded her head and gave a sad smile.

'That's amazing!' Missy's face beamed with happiness. 'You're my idol!'

Curie, Bell and Heisenberg — they're worthy idols, thought Felix. *But a cold-blooded killer?*

Missy's smile slipped. 'Why do you have to keep your identity a secret?'

'I grew up on a farm,' Attilia began to explain.

'Lucky you,' Lucius said. 'Being a farmer is my dream job. But what does that have to do with being a gladiator?'

Attilia smiled at Lucius before continuing. 'As soon as I was old enough to help the horses plough the fields I was put to work from dawn to dusk.

I grew strong – very strong. By the age of ten I could pull a plough five times my weight and lift a cart full of apples above my head. People in my village used to pick on me for being strong, as if it were a sin. But being a strong woman is nothing to be ashamed of.'

'Absolutely!' agreed Missy.

'I was determined to show everyone that my strength would not be my weakness – that it should be celebrated and applauded. So on my eighteenth birthday I left home with nothing but the clothes on my back and a few bronze coins in my pocket. I came to Rome to seek my fortune.'

'Did you go to gladiator school?' Lucius asked. 'Like us?'

Attilia shook her head. 'No. I wish I had done. If I'd been to gladiator school then I could have trained as a girl, as a gladiatrix, and everyone would have known from the very start just who I am. But I thought I knew better than anyone else, even the guards and instructors at the schools. So I came straight here, to the gladiators' barracks. I banged on the gates early one morning and begged them to let me in, but they wouldn't. They said that this was where the very best gladiators lived – it was no place for a woman. But I was determined to prove them wrong. I came back the next day, only this time I disguised myself as a man. I used the bronze coins I had to buy some wooden armour, which hid my body. I tied my hair up in a tight knot, hidden beneath a simple wooden helmet. This time the guards opened the gates to me, but they said I couldn't stay unless I fought for my place here.'

'So what happened?' Felix asked impatiently.

'I fought, and I won, of course.' Attilia shrugged at the memory. 'It wasn't a fight to the death. All I had to do was overpower Cranius – the most vicious gladiator here at the time.'

'I remember Cranius,' Lucius said eagerly. 'He was the most brutal gladiator in Rome before you came along, Attilius . . . I mean, Attilia.'

'It only took three blows for me to win the fight,' Attilia continued. 'My plan was to take off my helmet and armour as soon as I had won – to reveal my true identity and win my place here in the gladiator barracks. But I hadn't known that Emperor Nero had been watching the fight in the barracks courtyard from a window in his palace.'

'What happened?'

'Nero shouted down for the guards to seize me and bring me straight to him – before I had the chance to reveal my identity. My hands were cuffed and I was escorted into the royal palace to stand in front of the great Emperor Nero.'

'You don't have to call him "great" around us,' Felix said. 'We're not your average Roman citizens – we know how stupid and evil he actually is.'

'Yeah,' agreed Lucius. 'We've all heard the tale about the time he ordered every temple in the city to sacrifice two hundred goats because he had an ingrown toenail.'

Attilia snorted with amusement. 'Nero asked the guards to leave, and he and I were alone. He asked me to remove my helmet. He seemed shocked at first that I was a woman, although he said he had suspected as much all along—'

Felix chuckled. 'Yeah, right . . .'

'Nero told me that with training and time I would be the most incredible gladiator that Rome had ever seen. He told me that I would be his very own "personal project" – he would oversee my image, my skill set, my career. He would make me into a living legend. All I had to do was agree to disguise myself as a man.'

'Why?' Missy asked angrily. 'There's nothing wrong with being a woman – being a gladiatrix who fights better than anyone else.'

'I know that.' Attilia smiled. 'And maybe one day . . . years from now . . . other people will agree.'

'They will,' Missy said with absolute certainty.

'But right now, people don't think like that. Yes, some women do fight – but not as well as me. For my strength and courage to be truly celebrated, people have to think I'm a man.'

'That's really sad,' Felix said.

'And annoying,' Missy added. 'Not to mention wrong, unfair, stupid and old-fashioned.'

'How long did you have to train for?' Lucius asked. 'Before they let you fight for real, in the arena?'

'Not long,' Attilia replied. 'I was more or less battle-ready as soon as I arrived in Rome. What took time was creating this.' She pointed to her marvellous golden helmet. 'Nero said that to be a true legend, I needed more than just strength. I needed the object of legends . . . So he had this made. The gold was brought in from Persia and moulded to my exact specifications, designed so not a slip of my skin or face could be seen. Nero gave me the armour and the weapons too. I thought he was being kind. But Nero doesn't know how to be kind. What I realize now is that he was making me into his slave – by giving me these things, by changing me from Attilia to Attilius, he was chaining me to him. I was no longer free. I belonged to him.'

'And now you can only be free again if you carry on killing?'

Attilia nodded sadly. 'The first time I stepped foot in the arena, I knew I would never forgive myself. But I have no choice. If I don't fight for Nero then I will never be free again. Every fight he promises will be my last, but it never is. However, there's a fight coming up, a big one – and if I win that then Nero has sworn to the gods that he will give me my freedom.'

'You believe him?'

She shrugged sadly. 'What choice do I have?'

'What do you know about this fight?' Felix asked. 'Can you win it?'

'I have to fight and slaughter every child in the city's gladiator school,' she said, her voice suddenly cold.

Lucius turned to Felix, a look of horror etched on his face. 'That means . . . that she's fighting us. But that's impossible! We haven't even graduated yet – some of us are too small to hold a proper sword!'

'You won't have to worry about holding a sword.' Attilia hung her head, ashamed. 'None of you will be allowed to carry a weapon into the arena.'

'Lambs to the slaughter,' Felix said. 'And that's why we're here, Attilia – we want to convince you not to kill us. We're all students at the city's gladiator school. Take a good long look at our faces – it's us you'll be murdering.'

Attilia turned away then. 'You don't know what it is you're asking of me. If I don't kill you all then I'll never be free. And you shouldn't have come here – to know the face of those you kill . . .' she turned and looked at them again, 'is torture.'

'So don't kill us,' Missy pleaded, taking a step towards Attilia.

'It's kill or be killed, you know that,' Attilia snapped back.

'But what if we can find another way?' Felix said quickly. 'If I can find a way to let you win the fight without landing a single blow on one of us, would you let me? Just trust me – I'll find a way. I promise.'

Attilia held her head in her hands. 'If I don't win this fight then I'll never be free. All my life, all I ever wanted was to be a gladiator. But now all I want is my freedom. Finally, this is my chance. Nero has promised me a fortune when I retire. I'll use my money to leave this city and never come back. All my hopes and dreams are riding on this one last fight. Why should I trust you?'

'The fight might be your chance of freedom,'

Felix said, choosing his words carefully, 'but trusting me is your chance to show the world that you're not a monstrous killer. You're just . . . misunderstood.'

'I *am* misunderstood,' Attilia agreed. 'I'm a good person.'

Hmm, I'm not sure good people ever think it's OK to kill people — freedom or no freedom, thought Felix. He didn't say anything aloud.

'If there was a way for us all to step into the arena and leave it as living, free citizens of Rome then I'd take it in a heartbeat,' Attilia added.

'I'll find a way,' Felix assured her. 'Once I've got a plan in place then I'll send word to you. I promise.'

Attilia nodded. 'The fight is two full moons from now. I'll wait to hear from you, young gladiator. But if I don't then I shall see you in the arena, be ready.'

'We will be,' Felix promised.

They left Attilia alone and crept through the barracks, back to the world outside.

'Now we just need to figure out how Attilia ca

win the fight without killing us,' Lucius pointed out.

'That's not all we need to figure out . . .' Missy whispered to Felix, so Lucius couldn't hear. 'The skeleton found wearing Attilia's armour was a man.'

'You're sure about that?' Felix asked.

'You're questioning modern science?' Missy frowned.

'Of course not,' Felix said quickly. 'You're right. If the skeleton is a man then it can't belong to Attilia. So who was it? And how did that man end up with Attilia's armour? I'm not sure we're any closer to finding out the truth than we ever were . . .'

13
The Truth

When Felix, Missy and Lucius arrived back at the school gates they were closed and locked up.

'I can't see any guards,' Missy whispered, peering through the iron bars. 'If they'd noticed we were missing the place would be crawling with them. We could climb over the gates?'

'Or we could pick the lock?' Lucius suggested.

'Let's not risk it,' Felix said, rummaging around in his bag. 'I have a better idea.'

Felix felt Einstein scurry down his arm before hopping on to the metal gate. The little lizard lifted one of his front legs and waved it towards the straps of Felix's backpack.

'I know what you're thinking, little guy,' Felix

muttered. He pulled out a roll of copper wire and a nine-volt battery from his bag. 'Just the tool for the job . . .'

An electromagnet!

How to make an electromagnet:

1. Wrap copper wire tightly around an iron nail.

2. Attach the end of the wire to a battery.

3. Hey presto! You've created an electromagnet!

4. The tighter you wind the wire . . . the stronger the magnet will be!

Felix looked down, his gaze roaming over the cobbles and dirt until he found what he was looking for. 'Ah-ha!' He picked up a rusted old iron nail.

'You're making an electromagnet?' Missy asked, surprised.

'A what-a-what?' Lucius frowned.

'An electromagnet.' Felix nodded. 'I just need to wind the copper wire tightly around the nail . . . attach the wire ends to the battery . . . and . . .'

Felix held the nail, wrapped in copper wire, to the gate lock. Slowly, he used the super-strength electromagnet to slide the lock open.

'We're in!' He pushed the gate open carefully and ushered Missy and Lucius inside. Einstein leaped back on to his shoulder, glowing a mellow **yellow** in relief.

'If the guards see you with those tools you'll be crucified,' Lucius said, sounding worried. 'You know that, right?'

'That's why we need to sneak into the dorm and into our beds before the guards see us.' Missy pushed Lucius across the courtyard, towards the dormitory.

The three children crept inside. Flaming torches burned along the walls, and most of the children were fast asleep.

'Don't think I didn't notice you were gone today, maggots,' came a voice from one of the mattresses.

Felix looked down as he walked towards his own mattress. '*You* might have a gut of steel, Domitius, but we spent the afternoon in the medical hut vomiting up this morning's stuffed rat.'

Domitius snorted proudly. 'I do have a gut of steel.'

'We should get our heads down,' Lucius whispered to Felix and Missy. 'Just go to sleep. Don't draw any more attention to ourselves this evening . . .'

* * *

In the dead of night, Felix bent down and placed Einstein on Missy's face. The lizard waddled across her cheek and used his tiny foot to tickle behind her ear. Missy's eyes flew open and the next thing she knew Felix had his hand clapped over her mouth to silence her.

'Don't scream,' he whispered. 'I need to speak to you. Outside, now.'

Missy pulled herself out of bed and followed Felix to the other end of the dormitory, past the rows of sleeping bodies on either side. They stepped out into the cold Rome night air. Einstein perched on Missy's shoulder. She glanced down at him nervously; she wasn't used to having the small reptile sitting on her.

'I think we should go home,' Felix said as soon as the dorm door was closed behind them.

'What? Why?' Missy asked, confused. 'You heard Attilia today – if we can find a plan that wins her freedom and doesn't involve killing then she'll go along with it . . .'

'I know, I know.' Felix rubbed his tired eyes. He hadn't had a wink of sleep since they'd got back. 'And I know I said I'd come up with a plan—'

'You promised you would,' Missy reminded him.

'I've been lying awake all night trying to think of something.' Felix forced himself not to shout with frustration. 'But I can't ignore the fact that any plan will disrupt the space-time continuum.'

'Er . . . come again?'

'Stopping Attilia from killing everyone will change the course of history.'

Felix rubbed at his temples, frustrated. In one hand he held the old TV remote control. The co-ordinates of his bedroom and the time and date of the moment he and Missy had left were already programmed in. All he needed to do was press the green button and they'd be whizzing forward in time . . .

'Science fiction is full of stories of people who travel back in time, change the course of history and disrupt the space-time continuum. If we stop Attilia killing Lucius, then we'll stop her earning her freedom. The skeleton in the garden is a man – it isn't Attilia. Who knows who it is?'

Missy took a deep breath. 'We're not leaving now, Felix. We came here to do a job, remember? What about your signature on the helmet, what about saving Lucius – do you really just want to stand back and let him be killed again?'

'Killed again?' came Lucius's voice. He stepped out of the shadows, his eyes wide with terror and confusion. 'What do you mean?'

'Lucius . . .' Missy began to backtrack. 'What Felix meant was—'

'I know what he meant,' Lucius snapped. 'I heard everything you said. I saw you both getting out of bed and coming outside so I followed you. You can't think of a plan so you're just going to give up. You're going to let Attilia win her freedom by killing us . . . you think we're all going to die. No . . .' Lucius paused before adding. 'You *know* we're going to die.'

'Lucius, I'm so sorry.' Felix hung his head. 'I came back here because I wanted to help you. I can't—'

'What do you mean you "came back here"?'

'Um . . . well . . . he's been to Rome once before and . . .' Missy for once struggled to find the right words.

'You're lying,' Lucius said with certainty. 'You two have done nothing but lie to me ever since you arrived. I know you're not from Rome. I don't think you're even from the Roman Empire. Please just tell me the truth,' he demanded.

Felix's imagination went into overdrive as he tried to conjure up some kind of excuse . . .

We're secret assassins sent to kill Attilia.

We're not really here, we're figments of your imagination.

We're just a couple of rich kids playing at being gladiators.

We're actually aliens!

'The truth is that we're time travellers,' Missy said simply.

Oh, lab rats! Not the truth! Anything but the truth!

They both looked at Lucius, waiting for some kind of reaction. But Lucius's face remained as still as stone.

'We're from the future,' Missy added gently. 'We came back to find out more about Attilia. We also thought that maybe we could help you—'

'How do you know I get killed by Attilia?' Lucius asked. 'How do you know I don't go on to become a great warrior myself one day?'

Oh, vomiting vinegar volcanoes! I don't think I can lie myself out of this one, not any more, thought Felix. *It's time for the truth, the whole truth and nothing but the truth. Here goes . . .*

'This isn't the first time I've come back in time,' Felix said carefully.

Lucius let out a nervous chuckle. 'I don't understand . . .'

Felix tried to explain everything. 'It all started when I used an old microwave to build a teleportation machine—'

'Microwave? Teleportation machine? What are they?' Lucius asked, confused.

'But what I was trying to build didn't work as I'd planned,' Felix said, skipping over any kind of explanation of microwave or teleportation machine. 'The machine took me back in time. It transported me nearly two thousand years into the past, back here to Rome. And I met you – you were heading into the arena to fight Attilia. This fight that's coming up, where she must fight every child in the school for her freedom – I can't stop it. I'd be changing the course of history. I'm sorry—'

'No.' Lucius shook his head. 'Don't tell me you're sorry. You have to help us. Please! Help us!'

'He's right, Felix,' Missy agreed. 'We can find a way to avoid changing the course of history and still save everyone – I know we can.'

'Whoever you are, Felix,' Lucius pleaded, 'if one person can help us, it's you. Everything you did today – creating a diversion and sneaking us out of school, then sneaking us back in with that magnet thingy – you're amazing. Please help us, Felix. Please just try. I'll do anything in return, anything.'

'I don't want anything,' Felix replied. 'It's the space-time continuum—'

'That's the stuff of science fiction, Felix!' Missy threw her hands into the air.

'You have to help me!' Lucius grabbed Felix's shoulders and looked into his eyes, pleadingly.

Felix's neurons fired off a billion and one thoughts all at once . . .

I could press the green button now.

I could take Lucius with us.

Rescue him from his terrible fate.

But Lucius is meant to live and die in Ancient Rome.

I can't meddle with history.

Maybe Missy's right (although I'll never admit it to her face!).

Maybe there is a way to help . . .

'Please,' Lucius begged once again, his eyes glistening with tears. 'I don't want to die in Nero's Arena. I want to grow old and grey and die on my farm. Please.'

'OK,' Felix agreed. 'We'll stay. But if we do this – if we change the course of history – then you need to know the risks.' Both Missy and Lucius eagerly nodded their heads. 'If the space-time continuum is disrupted, if history doesn't play out the way that it's meant to, then life as we know it could change. Nothing may ever be the same again.'

14
Changing History

ATTILIVS'S
FINAL FIGHT
FOR FREEDOM

ATTILIVS
VERSVS
THE MARS ACADEMY

MAIVS XII
NERO'S ARENA

The poster had been nailed to every wall in the gladiator school while the children slept. Talk of the fight was all Felix could hear when he woke the next morning.

'We can't fight yet – we haven't finished training!'

'Whoever lands the killer blow on Attilius will go down in the history books!'

'I heard he's blind in one eye . . .'

'What if the gods intervene – maybe we'll all be saved?'

'Nero may as well have handed us all a death sentence.'

Even Domitius was paler than usual.

'I don't know why you seem so calm, maggot,' Domitius snarled at Felix during fight practice that morning. 'You'll be the first to die at Attilius's sword.'

'Maybe I've made peace with the god of death,' Felix mumbled back. *Or maybe I'm too busy trying to come up some kind of plan to save your backside! There's just so much to think about . . .*

How can Attilia win her freedom without killing a single one of us?

If the bones of the murdered gladiator don't belong to Attilia, then whose are they?

How did that murdered gladiator, whoever he was, end up with Lucius's ring, Domitius's belt buckle and a fortune of gold coins?

I didn't engrave my signature into Attilia's helmet last night, so how did it get there?

* * *

'The poster says May the 12th,' Lucius pointed out as they sat down to eat a lunch of stuffed sparrow. 'Two months' time – just like Attilia said it would be.'

'Two months is loads of time to think of a plan to knock the socks off Attilia.' Felix smiled confidently. 'I've got a few ideas I'm considering at the moment . . .' *None of which seem at all possible*, he said to himself. 'But they still need some work. Two months should be plenty of time.'

'*Should* be plenty of time?' Lucius pointed out. 'What if it isn't?'

'Then we have two months to get you battle-ready,' Missy replied.

'That's not enough time.' Lucius shook his head. 'I can't even see from one side of the arena to the other – how am I meant to fight someone like Attilia?'

'Well the eyesight is definitely something I can help you with.' Felix grinned.

Before they spent the afternoon darning holes in the guards' pants and polishing spearheads, Felix slipped back to the dormitory and rifled through his backpack.

He pulled out his trusty safety goggles.

'These have served me well, Einstein,' he said to his pet lizard, who nibbled hungrily at the scraps of stuffed sparrow Felix had brought him. 'But now they have a new purpose . . . I'm going to make Lucius a pair of glasses. Though without the equipment in my bedroom laboratory I'd never be able to create a pair of glasses in an afternoon – thank Jupiter we have two months until the fight! And speaking of the fight . . . I have a few other ideas to help us all get battle-ready.'

Einstein swallowed down the last of his sparrow and changed his scales to **orange**.

'Don't worry, buddy,' Felix reassured him. 'I'm hoping we won't have to fight Attilia at all. I'm hoping I'll spend the next two months coming up with a razor-sharp plan to win Attilia's freedom and save the lives of every child in the school, solving the mystery of the two-thousand-year-old murdered gladiator in the process. But if all else fails, then we need a plan B.'

Before he left the dorm, Felix pulled his pen and

pencil from his bag and scribbled down a few of his ideas to show the others.

Felix handed one piece of paper to Missy as they sat around fixing the guards' crusty old pants that afternoon.

Fighting Formula
$$e + m + s + c + f + of = ug$$

Missy took one look at Felix's equation and raised her eyebrows, looking at him for an explanation.

'Isn't it obvious?' Felix sighed, frustrated.

'Not to someone who's not a genius,' Missy replied.

Felix shook his head. He wrote down an explanation on the paper.

energy (food!) + mass (child) + speed + co-ordination + force + other factors = ultimate gladiator

'What are the other factors?' Missy asked.

'Things like wind,' Felix replied. 'It might seem

insignificant but having a gust of wind on your side just might be the difference between making your net fly that extra centimetre through the air.'

'So we should always try to fight with the wind behind us,' Missy concluded.

'Exactly.'

'And what about these things here?' She pointed to 'Speed', 'Co-ordination', 'Force' and 'Mass'.

'The greater the mass, the more force it will have behind it.'

'So we should all weigh more?' Missy looked confused.

'Yes, but we should bulk out our weight in muscles, not fat. And a higher muscle tone will help with S. Speed. The stronger and more powerful our muscles are, the more speed we'll be able to propel our bodies forward with.'

'Got it – strong arms and legs. I know a few exercises from my mum's fitness magazines that will help us. But what about co-ordination?'

Felix looked over at Lucius as he jammed his needle into his finger.

'Let's just hope that co-ordination is something

that can be taught . . . otherwise we'll just have to rely on the other elements of the formula to create the ultimate gladiator.'

Lucius sucked on his bleeding finger and frowned. 'What other ideas have you had?' he asked. Missy turned the piece of paper over.

Training Schedule

Weeks 1-2: Basic fitness work (cardio – running, star jumps, skipping ropes).

Weeks 3-4: Fitness work and muscle-building (lifting light weights, sit-ups, press-ups, chin-ups).

Weeks 5-6: Fitness and muscle work (heavier weights now!), battle strategy and weapon practice!

Weeks 7-8: Fitness, strength, strategy, weapons and fight practice!

'Training schedule?' Lucius looked dubious.

'Two months,' Felix said with a deep breath. 'Eight weeks. Sixty days. We have approximately eight hours a day outside of basic gladiator training that we can use for our extra training. That's four hundred and eighty hours of intensive, uninterrupted, concentrated, full-throttle fight training. We have two months to get battle-ready, if we need to resort to plan B.'

'Plan B?'

'Fighting to the death,' Missy replied. Lucius looked horrified. 'Don't worry, we're hoping it won't come to that. But if it does . . . If all else fails us . . . If science fails us—'

'Science never fails anybody,' Felix said quickly.

* * *

The next few days passed in a blur of chin-ups, running and star jumps. They fell asleep bone-tired each night, their muscles aching from the day's training. Every morning Einstein woke Felix up by pulling at his ear. Who needs an alarm clock when you have a pet lizard? The days passed into weeks . . .

And the weeks began to slip by . . .

With every passing day each one of them noticed that they could run further without stopping, and their muscles hurt less.

Every week they grew stronger, and soon some of their classmates began joining the training sessions.

On the first day of the third week, as they crept out of the dormitory before dawn, Livia, a small girl from their dormitory, followed them outside. 'You've been doing some extra training,' she said to Felix. 'I want to join in too.'

Felix smiled. 'The more the merrier.'

On the second day of the third week, Livia's best friend Octavia joined in. And the next day a boy called Augustus also came along. After a month they had another ten students waking up early and running laps of the courtyard with them.

'Do we need to worry about this lot?' snarled one guard to another.

'I wouldn't bother,' said the second guard. 'Let them do whatever makes them happy. Soon enough they'll all be in the arena and Attilius will slaughter them all. Makes no difference what they do now – they'll never survive.'

Week six arrived and Domitius approached Felix over lunch that day.

'This little out-of-hours school club you've started,' Domitius said, shifting his weight from one foot to another, 'totally lame. It looks like you need someone with my level of experience to help out . . .'

'Are you saying you want to join in with our extra training?' Missy asked.

'No, worm-head,' Domitius replied. 'I'm saying I want to lead it.'

'You can't.' Felix shook his head. 'But I'm not going to stop you joining in, if that's what you want. Every one of us needs a fair shot in the arena – I won't get in your way of doing extra training. But you're a few weeks behind the rest of us . . .'

'And you're a lifetime behind me, maggot-face.'

'Charming,' Felix muttered to himself as Domitius waddled away.

'Maggot-face,' Missy said to Felix. 'I'm sure I heard Derek say something similar to me once . . .'

She's right, Felix thought, looking down, ashamed. *And he's said worse things behind her back . . .*

The training continued the next day, and the next.

It started paying off – in battle lessons the children were becoming faster, sharper, stronger. Swords felt lighter in their hands. They could whip nets at their opponents faster, block blows quicker with their shields, and duck and dive from punches in the blink of an eye.

'Felix,' Missy said, as the last week of training arrived. 'All this preparation has been amazing. We're stronger, faster, sharper and more skilled with our weapons than ever. This is as good as a plan B is ever going to get.' Felix smiled back at her. 'But what about plan A?' A look of concern clouded her face. 'All these weeks have gone by and you've

183

not mentioned it once. You're not just relying on plan B, are you? We're strong, but I still don't fancy our chances against Attilia, and even if we could overpower her, I don't think I really want to kill—'

'Don't worry.' Felix smiled confidently. 'I have it all worked out. Trust me . . .' He nodded towards the back of the dormitory, and Missy followed him. Einstein was sitting on Felix's bed, his scales shimmering **red**.

'Why is Einstein flashing red for danger?' asked Missy, who now knew all of the chameleon's colours and what they meant.

'I'm sending him out on a mission,' Felix whispered. He reached into his bag, pulled out a small notepad and pen, and scribbled something down. 'He's smuggling a note to Attilia.'

'Saying what?'

Felix passed the note to Missy.

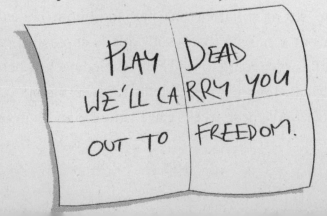

15
Plan A

The night before the big fight, Felix presented Lucius with the pair of glasses he'd spent the last two months creating.

'I took some natron – baking soda,' he reminded Missy. 'The white powder we used to make vinegar volcanoes. Made it into a paste, and used it to grind the glass from my safety goggles into convex lenses. Then I used some wire scraps to make a basic frame for the lenses to sit in. Try them on.' He handed the homemade glasses to Lucius. 'The lenses will bend the light entering your eye, and rectify your eyesight.'

Lucius gasped as he put the glasses on. 'Incredible! Look at the detail around us . . . look at the dust on the ground, the grime up the walls, the spiders weaving their webs above our beds. It's amazing . . . it's . . . actually really disgusting! Why has no one pointed out how revolting everything around us actually is before? I think I was better off not being able to see properly . . .'

'Nonsense,' Felix said, grinning. 'You'll be able to spot every twitch of Attilia's muscles now. And, speaking of Attilia, we should all get our heads down. We need every minute of sleep we can get for our cells to regenerate and strengthen before tomorrow.'

Felix saw Missy and Lucius exchange a very worried glance as he lay down on his mattress and closed his eyes.

'He said we need to trust him,' Felix heard Missy whisper.

Felix lay awake with his eyes closed, staying that way for hours until he could hear Lucius snoring. Hoping that everyone else in the dormitory was asleep, Felix slowly sat up in bed. Einstein crawled on to his shoulder as Felix got up and walked towards Missy's mattress. He bent down and prodded her.

Missy woke up with a snort.

Felix pointed to Missy's rucksack, mouthed, 'Gold coins,' at her, then pointed at the dormitory door. Missy nodded at him.

In a moment they were both standing outside under a full moon. In Missy's hands she held the last of the Roman gold coins she'd brought back in time with them.

'Is this where you tell me your plan A?' Missy said hopefully. 'You want Attilia to play dead so we can carry her out. But then what?'

'Relax!' Felix shrugged. 'It's all up here . . .' He tapped at his head.

'Then why did you wake me up?' Missy narrowed her eyes. 'I need my sleep if I'm going to fight to the death in front of thousands of Romans tomorrow.'

'No one's fighting to the death tomorrow. I need you to trust me, remember?' Missy rolled her eyes at Felix. 'Follow me . . .'

Felix led Missy towards the school gates in silence. After two months of intensive training Felix was so strong that he lifted himself up and over the iron gates without any effort whatsoever, and Missy followed closely behind.

Without making a sound, Felix and Missy ran through the cobbled Roman streets.

I'm actually going to miss this place when we go home, he thought to himself. *If we ever get home . . . If just one thing goes wrong tomorrow then the whole plan will fail . . .*

They ran along streets, down winding alleyways, past sleeping beggars and stray dogs and countless shrines to the many Roman gods. Eventually, Felix stopped and stood outside a small shop.

'A bakery?' Missy said as she looked up at the shop sign.

Felix nodded. 'We're going to sneak in, take as many sacks of cornflour as we can carry and replace it with a gold coin.'

Missy stared at Felix for a long moment, before finally asking, 'Why?'

'Quicksand,' Felix said, and he disappeared into the bakery.

Missy said something under her breath about feeding Felix to a pack of hungry Roman vultures as she followed him in. All of the bakers were at home in bed. There wasn't a single candle burning, and only the light from the full moon illuminated the shop.

It didn't take long to find the sacks of cornflour. They were each able to carry three large sacks, and Missy placed a gold coin on the bakery counter. 'That's more than enough for the flour,' she reassured Felix. 'Now what? Go back to school and make the quicksand there? Why? What do we need it for?'

'Now we carry the sacks to the arena,' was all Felix said.

The arena wasn't far, but Felix's arms and back were stiff and sore by the time they arrived. Felix knew Missy was far too stubborn to ever complain, but she must have been aching too.

They threw the sacks of cornflour, one by one, over the arena gates. Then they climbed the gates and stood inside the arena.

'And now?' Missy panted.

Felix walked into the empty arena and looked around.

Moonlight bounced off of the stone seats, and Felix was struck by just how magnificent the arena really was. For a moment, he forgot about why they were there and what they needed to do.

The architecture of this place is phenomenal. The skill, the engineering, the craftsmanship involved in creating such a structure! If thousands of people and animals hadn't been slaughtered here then I'd think this place was as beautiful as the aurora . . .

'Felix!' Missy shouted, her voice echoing off the empty stone seats.

'Right,' Felix muttered. 'If Attilia enters the arena on a chariot from that entrance there . . .' he turned towards the far gate, 'and is travelling at ten miles per hour . . . and we need approximately one minute to get every child into the arena and in position, the chariot will be right about . . .' he ran towards a spot in the arena, 'here.' He gestured for Missy to start bringing the bags of cornflour over to where he stood. 'We need to empty the flour into this spot.'

'Why—' Missy began to ask before rolling her eyes in frustration. 'I should trust you, I know.'

Felix nodded and the two of them got to work emptying out the bags of cornflour on to the arena floor.

'What next?' Missy asked.

'Now we go to every other bakery in the city to get more cornflour, and we come back here and empty out the bags on to the arena ground, using this spot as the centre of the radius.'

Missy didn't ask a single question as she and Felix spent the rest of the night running around the city, visiting bakery after bakery. They carried as many bags of cornflour into the arena as they could, leaving a gold coin behind each time as payment, until the coins had gone and the sun was beginning to creep over the horizon. As they left the arena for the last time, they covered the flour with a thin layer of dirt to hide it.

'So let me guess,' Missy said, sounding exhausted, as they walked back towards the school. 'Tomorrow, when Attilia rides into the arena on her chariot, we'll turn the cornflour on the ground into quicksand and stop her in her tracks.'

Felix smiled. 'See, you didn't need me to explain a thing.'

'And then we pretend to kill Attilia, and once her body's been carried out of the arena we somehow sneak her off to freedom.' Missy bit down on her lip, looking concerned. 'It's a good plan, Felix . . . but what makes you think Nero will just let you kill his prized gladiator?'

'Nero's not in the ring with us.' Felix shrugged. *What's her point?* he thought.

'No, but whether a gladiator lives or dies is ultimately the emperor's call. You can't land the killer blow without his permission. And something tells me he'll never let a school kid take out the most famous gladiator Rome's ever seen.'

Er, this is not what I want to be hearing right now! 'Got a better idea, Missy?' he said out loud.

193

'No,' she replied honestly. 'But maybe if we expose who Attilia really is,' she said thoughtfully, 'maybe if the Romans find out she's been lying to them the whole time, then Nero will let us kill her – fake kill her – to keep everyone happy. But how can we show everyone that she's really a woman?'

Felix had an idea . . . 'Leave that to me.'

The cock was beginning to crow as they pulled themselves up and over the school gates.

'Nothing will go wrong,' Felix reassured Missy, though his voice didn't sound as sure.

Missy rubbed at her eyes as they crossed the courtyard towards the dormitory. 'I don't fancy dying today.'

'What were you guys doing outside?' Lucius asked, as they sneaked back into the dorm. 'I thought we all agreed we wouldn't do our early morning run today – we're saving all our energy and strength for the big fight.'

'We weren't running,' Felix explained, picking up his bag and swinging it over his shoulder. 'We were putting plan A into action.'

'Plan A?' Lucius said. 'What do we need to do?'

'Nothing,' Missy told him. 'Just focus on the fight and everything we've done in training. If plan A fails then you'll need to fight for your life.'

'It won't fail,' Felix said with certainty. 'By this time tomorrow Attilia will be free and we'll be on our way home.'

'And if it doesn't work, and Attilia is too strong for us all?' Lucius asked nervously. 'What's plan C?'

Felix fell silent and looked away.

It won't fail . . . it can't fail . . . can it?

16
Fight Day, Take Two

The procession from the gladiator school to Nero's Arena was exactly the same as it had been the first time Felix had joined it. Exactly the same apart from two things:

1. Inside Felix's backpack was his homemade electromagnet. Before they'd left the school that morning he'd spent an hour winding the copper wire as tightly as he could around the old nail, making the magnet super-strong.

2. Felix had persuaded the guards to let every child take a large clay jug from the school. 'The sun is roasting today,' he argued. 'You don't want us to die of thirst before we even get to the arena.'

'We can fill the jugs up with water from the fountains on the street,' Felix had told everyone, thinking of the free water fountains dotted around Rome. 'Fill your jugs to the brim and carry them with you into the arena.'

'How can we fight Attilius with water jugs in our hands?' Domitius had argued.

'By the time we need to fight, the jugs will be empty, and our hands will be free,' was all Felix replied.

Dressed in red togas, the colour of sacrifice, Felix had learned, the children walked through the busy Roman streets in silence, just like before.

There must have been over one hundred children from the school in total. Each one seemed lost in their own thoughts. Felix could only imagine what might be going through their minds . . .

If I die today I'll be greeted in the underworld by my ancestors with pride.

If I could land one blow, just one blow before I die . . .

I won't die today. I won't die today. I won't die today.

Someone's got to kill Attilius one day — it may as well be me.

We don't stand a chance — not one of us will be alive by sunset.

'Here you are.' One of the guards pointed at an ornate drinking fountain on the side of the street. 'Take it in turns to fill up your water jugs. If you're going to die today then at least you won't die thirsty.'

'Everyone's so preoccupied with the fight.' Missy nudged Felix in the ribs as she queued up behind him. 'No one's even noticed how strange it is that we're taking so much water into the arena.'

Felix didn't say anything. He filled his water jug to the brim, careful not to spill a single drop.

'Felix!' Missy shook her head, beginning to look nervous. The guards led them away from the fountain and past the hordes of spectators queuing to get into the arena, and up to the large gates where the competitors entered. Missy stared at the heavy gates as they swung open. 'I really hope you know what you're doing.'

They were herded into the holding pen.

It's just like before, Felix thought with a gulp.

Only this time I know what to expect. This time I'm prepared.

Felix nudged his way through the crowd of children until he stood at the front, nearest the arena gate. He could hear the roar of the crowd behind it, and his throat tightened up at memory of the gates swinging open and Attilia riding towards him.

Hold it together, Felix. It's show time!

'Everyone!' he called out. He put his jug on the ground carefully and waved his hands in the air. 'Everyone!'

The terrified children all turned and stared at Felix.

'We've spent the last two months preparing for this moment,' Felix said, the chants of the crowd and his own heartbeat pounding in his ears. 'Don't forget everything we've learned. Remember to be brave, be strong and be fast.'

Livia pushed her way towards Felix. 'But Attilius is braver and stronger and faster than all of us.'

There was a murmur of agreement from the others.

'But there's one of him,' Felix reminded them,

'and over a hundred of us. If we work together, then I know we can win this. Remember the fight tactics we learned – teamwork is important, and it's all we really have on our side.'

'Slaughter him!' Domitius shouted. 'Cut him down to a bloody stump!'

'No!' Felix quickly shouted. 'There's a way to win this without shedding blood.' Felix crouched down and began to draw shapes in the dusty ground with his finger. 'This is the gate that Attilius's chariot will come through. And this is the path he'll take through the arena. We only have a minute to get into position and surround him.' Felix drew a semicircle. 'We must stand side by side, surrounding Attilius. And when I give you the sign we must all throw our water jugs at the ground.'

'Why?' Domitius asked.

'Because it's the only plan we have,' Felix answered, honestly.

'ATTILIUS! ATTILIUS! BLOOD AND GLORY BE HIS NAME.

ATTILIUS! ATTILIUS! SMITE AND BLOW AND MAIM.

Attilius! Attilius! Slaughterer of babes.
Attilius! Attilius! Golden helmet,
shining blade.'

The sound of the crowd was deafening. The children hugged their water jugs to their chests in desperation as the seconds ticked by and their reckoning time came closer.

The heavy wooden gates rattled on their hinges.

'It's time,' Lucius whispered. He turned to the others, and with his free hand he gave them the Roman salute. 'For the glory of the Empire. May the gods be with you.'

'For the glory of the Empire!' every child shouted, giving Lucius a salute right back.

The heavy gates slowly creaked open, pulled apart by two thick-armed Roman centurions.

Déjà vu! thought Felix. *This is exactly, exactly as it happened before . . .*

As the gates opened, the arena beyond loomed above Felix. The stadium was bursting with life, a multitude of colours and sounds. Streamers flew through the air, and people chanted for blood.

Thousands of fists pumped at the sky.

'**ATTILIUS! ATTILIUS! ATTILIUS!**'

Felix's feet began to move forward, into the arena. He spotted Nero on his throne across the stadium. His crown of golden leaves perched on top of his sweaty head, and a luxurious purple toga was draped across his bloated body. Slave children fanned Nero as he shoved handfuls of nuts into his greedy mouth.

Stay calm, focus, focus.

Felix knew that time was not on their side. He only had a minute to get everyone into position and set the wheels of his plan in motion. Two Roman soldiers began to pull apart the gate on the far side of the arena . . .

'Take up your positions!' Felix shouted at the others.

Attilia's golden chariot burst through the gates and the crowd erupted into deafening cheers. Felix's words were drowned out as he tried to shout instructions. 'Missy – everyone needs to stand in a semicircle around the cornflour!'

The golden chariot was pulled by two large bulls, and Attilia stood at the reigns like a king.

'Fan out!' Missy shouted, pointing manically at the places where they should stand. 'Shoulder to shoulder. Water jugs out in front of you. Focus! Teamwork, remember!'

'ATTILIUS! ATTILIUS! ATTILIUS!'

Attilia's chariot made a lap around the arena just as Felix had remembered it, and just as he'd calculated it would for his plan to work. In one hand Attilia held her large metal axe, and in the other her heavy shield. On her head sat the solid gold helmet.

'Silence!' Nero shouted, as Attilia's chariot began to slow down and travel towards the spot that Felix had calculated on the arena ground.

'Today Rome will witness one of the greatest games

ever played. Today Attilius fights for his freedom. If he manages to slaughter every child in the arena before the sand falls in the hourglass, then he will be a free man. If he does not, then he will fight again tomorrow, and again the next day and the next.'

Nero lifted the hourglass filled with golden sand.

'One . . . two . . . three!'

Attilia's chariot made the final part of its journey across the arena.

Just one more metre . . . nearly there . . . nearly . . .

'Everyone! Throw your water out in front of you!' Felix screamed.

Felix tipped the contents of his own jug on to the arena floor, and beside him Missy and Lucius did the same. Felix watched the ground closely as the water began to seep into the cornflour.

Felix quickly looked around at his fellow classmates, then back to the ground. *It's working!*

As he'd instructed, the children threw the water from their jugs out in front of them. The water glistened like diamonds in the midday sun as it flew through the air and splashed on to the ground –

the ground that Missy and Felix had spent hours covering with cornflour the night before. As the water seeped into the flour, every child turned to look at Felix, desperately awaiting their next instruction, as if the ground were about to magically swallow them all up and whisk them off to safety.

Attilia's chariot rolled into the semicircle and ground to a sticky halt. Within a few seconds the chariot and the bulls were glued to the spot.

Praise evolution! It's worked! Now all I need to do is jump on to the chariot and pretend to kill Attilia, thought Felix.

'Quicksand!' Missy screeched in delight. 'You do read your physics textbooks, Felix!'

'BOO! BOO! BOO!'

The crowd roared with disapproval as they realized their greatest gladiator was being outwitted.

Not beaten yet, Attilia leaped down from the chariot on to the arena ground. But her feet landed in the quicksand, gluing her to the spot. 'Felix! I got your message from the lizard.' No one else could hear her words over the roar of the crowd.

'I told you – we're all getting out of this arena alive!'

'In the name of the gods,' Domitius hollered at Felix. 'What have you done? What have we done? We've turned the ground into a swamp, and imprisoned Attilia! How is this going to help anyone?'

'This isn't over yet!' Felix shouted. **Next stage of the plan . . . I just need to expose Attilia for who she really is . . .**

There was no time to waste.

Felix swung his backpack off and pulled out his super-strength electromagnet.

He revved it up and pointed it at Attilia. Just as Felix had predicted, the metal armour covering her body began to pull towards him and she cried out in horror. 'Felix, what are you doing?'

'It's time you showed Rome who you really are!' Felix shouted back.

The armour began to rip from Attilia's body and hurtle towards Felix. 'Watch out!' he warned the others as her breastplate flew through the air and landed with a crash at Felix's feet.

Attilia let out a mighty roar as the electromagnet forced her golden helmet from her head. She tried desperately to grasp at it, but it slipped through her fingers. She tried to run after it as it flew away, but her feet were glued into the quicksand.

As the helmet sped towards Felix, the crowd let out shocked gasps.

'He's a she!'

'Attilius is Attilia!'

'She's been lying this whole time!'

'In the name of the gods!'

'What sorcery is this?'

Felix ripped the copper wire from the battery and instantly disabled the electromagnet. The armour and helmet clattered to the ground. He looked over to Emperor Nero, who was rising from his throne in panic, looking around the stadium at the thousands of angry Roman citizens who had just realized they had been lied to. Their hero was not who Nero had led them to believe.

Felix was so busy watching Nero, he didn't notice Domitius from the corner of his eye . . .

'For the glory of the Empire!' Domitius shouted as he threw his empty water jug to the ground, shattering it to pieces. He hopscotched on the broken clay pieces over the quicksand and leaped into the chariot. He climbed up into the front and lifted his arms into the air. 'Citizens of Rome. I am here to rid you of this imposter, this charlatan, this woman who has been lying to you all this time!'

'What's he doing?' Missy shouted to Felix.

'How in Newton's name should I know?' Felix shouted back.

Domitius reached down into the chariot and pulled out a bow and arrow from Attilia's weapon stash.

He loaded the arrow into the bow and held it into a firing position, aiming it at Attilia's head. Trapped in the quicksand, Attilia bravely opened her arms, surrendering to Domitius.

'Domitius, NO!' Missy screamed.

She threw her own clay jug at the ground, copying Domitius and hopping across the small islands of broken clay pieces until she too could leap on to the golden chariot. She launched herself on to Domitius's back and tried desperately to wrestle the bow and arrow from his grasp.

'I'm killing Attilia!' Domitius shouted. 'I am a hero!'

'She's unarmed!' Missy cried, trying frantically to prise the weapon from him. 'The gods will not favour you if you kill an unarmed opponent.'

'She was going to kill us all and we only had water jugs to fight with!' Domitius screamed.

The crowd were divided. Half of them were chanting, 'Kill, Kill, Kill!'

The other half chanted, 'Save, Save, Save!'

'I'm going to end her life!' Domitius screamed, pulling back the bow.

'Missy, stop him!' Felix pleaded.

With all her strength Missy pulled at the bow in Domitius's hands. Just as he let go of the string, freeing the arrow into the air, she managed to tug the weapon away from the direction of Attilia, diverting the arrow as it was released.

The arrow shot through the air.

It soared past Attilia without even grazing her, the arrowhead glinting in the sunlight.

Everyone held their breath as they watched the arrow fall through the sky, hurtling towards the ground and the small blond boy who stood directly in its path.

All Felix could do was stare in horror as the arrow landed in the middle of Lucius's chest.

Lucius fell backward with the blow.

With the arrow protruding from his small body, he lay as still as stone on the arena ground.

17
The Edge of the Empire

The roar of the crowd sounded like white noise in Felix's ears. He couldn't hear a word they were screaming. He couldn't pay attention to what Missy was shouting as she leaped from the chariot and darted over the broken clay to join him at Lucius's side.

All Felix could hear, as the world around him drowned in noise, was the sound of Lucius dying. He was gasping for breath, his chest making a horrible gurgling noise as he tried to breathe.

From behind his bottle-thick glasses, Lucius's gaze found Felix.

'Felix . . .' he rasped.

'Don't try to speak.' Felix ripped open Lucius's

tunic so he could get a better look at the wound. The arrow had hit him deep in the chest, but it seemed to have just missed his heart by a fraction. 'Just try to breathe,' Felix said calmly.

'Felix,' Missy said, her expression grave. 'We need to get him to a doctor.'

'They don't have doctors for gladiators,' Lucius whispered. 'We either live or we die.'

'We don't need a doctor,' Felix said, trying to sound confident. *Who am I kidding? If he doesn't get to an operating table soon he'll bleed to death!*

'I'll help you, Lucius,' Felix whispered, reaching into his backpack. 'I promise.' He pulled out his Swiss army knife and began cutting up his own toga. He carefully placed the material over Lucius's open wound to try to stop the flow of blood. 'Hold this down,' Felix told Missy. 'Apply as much pressure to the wound as possible. If the blood soaks through, don't remove the material, just cut off some of your own toga and use it to apply more pressure.'

Missy nodded, her face drained of all colour. 'Felix,' she said, trying to hold back her sobs. 'Domitius . . . look . . .'

Felix turned around and instantly got to his feet.

Domitius had pulled Attilia's sword from the chariot and raised it in the air, ready to land a fatal blow on the once-great gladiator.

'Domitius, no!' Felix cried, running towards them and leaping onto the piece of broken jug.

Domitius brought down his sword, and the metal sang as it cut through the air. Attilia closed her eyes and muttered silent prayers to the Roman gods.

She trusts us, Felix thought with horror. *She thinks we're going to pretend to kill her, but Domitius is going to kill her for real.*

Domitius stopped the blade centimetres from Attilia's throat. He looked over to Emperor Nero.

'Emperor Nero!' Domitius shouted, glee and pride bursting from every pore. 'Should this traitor live or die?'

The crowd erupted into a chorus of chanting: 'ATTILIA! ATTILIA! ATTILIA! DOMITIUS! DOMITIUS! DOMITIUS!'

'Silence!' Nero commanded. He rose to his feet and stepped down from his throne. His slaves moved with him, still fanning him as he walked down from the spectators' seats and into the arena. The crowd gasped as he began to walk over the dried blood on the arena ground, towards the chariot where Domitius and Attilia were locked in their death clinch.

'Citizens of Rome,' Nero shouted, a smug grin spreading across his pudgy face. 'It appears that we have a new champion. What is your name, boy?'

'Domitius, sir.' Domitius's fingers twitched around the sword.

'Domitius isn't a champion!' came a small voice from behind Felix. He turned around and, to his astonishment, he saw Livia – the smallest girl in the school – straightening her back and addressing Nero directly. 'If anyone is a champion then it's

Felix.' She pointed right at him. 'Felix was the one who came up with the plan to trap Attilia – he's the one who's been training us for today. Without him Domitius would never have lifted a sword to Attilia's throat.'

Nero's eyes narrowed as he looked Felix up and down. 'Is this true, boy? Is this . . .' he pointed at the quicksand and Attilia's armour lying in a heap on the ground, 'all because of you?'

'Yes,' Felix admitted. He could almost feel the hatred in Domitius's eyes burning into him as he spoke. 'But I don't want to be crowned a champion. All I want is to walk out of this arena with my life, and for Attilia to go free.'

'HOW DARE YOU?!' Nero bellowed. 'You insolent, ignorant, putrid little toad! You don't get to dictate who lives and who dies – you don't get to demand that the greatest gladiator Rome has ever seen should go free. I AM THE EMPEROR. Only I can decide. And why should I even let this fraud,' he pointed at Attilia, 'live? She has been lying to us all! Pretending to be a man when all along she was a woman!'

The crowd jeered and clapped.

'But you knew that!' Felix shouted at Nero. 'You knew Attilius was really a woman. You gave her that helmet – you made her into the legend she is. And she's a woman – so what? She'll still go down in the history books as the bravest, deadliest, most brutal gladiator Rome has ever seen.'

'SILENCE!' Nero lifted his hand out in front of him. He clenched his fist and stuck his thumb out to the side. 'I have heard enough from you. The time has come to decide whether I let Domitius kill Attilia. Now . . . what shall I decide?'

His thumb began to waver in the air. He turned around in a circle, looking up at the crowd as they shouted down at him.

'Kill her!'

'Spare her!'

I know how this works, Felix thought, holding his breath. There was nothing he could do but hope. *Thumbs up she lives. Thumbs down she dies.*

Nero continued to turn slowly, studying the people around him . . .

Attilia was stuck in the quicksand, unarmed and prepared to die.

Domitius loomed over Attilia from the chariot, sword pressed at her throat, ready to strike.

Missy hunched over Lucius's bleeding body, desperately trying to save his life.

Felix, the crowd and all the other children held their breath, waiting for Nero to make his decision.

Nero's thumb wobbled up and down . . . up and down . . . up . . . down . . . up . . . down . . .

Up.

The crowd went wild.

'Attilia will live!' Nero shouted. 'And she will be free. She has served Rome well these last few years. She has the strength and courage of the gods – and she shall be rewarded, in this life and the next.'

Felix sank to his knees in relief. **We did it!**

Domitius threw the sword to the ground in disgust and disappointment.

'You!' Nero pointed at Domitius. 'I want you to enrol at the gladiator barracks – now Attilia is free you'll be taking her place.'

Domitius's fists pumped at the air in joy.

Is his brain a nano? Doesn't he realize he's just been condemned to a life of slavery and brutal death?

Domitius jumped down from the chariot and leaped across the pieces of jugs on the quicksand towards Felix. He reached for his belt buckle, loosened it and tossed it at Lucius's feet. 'You'll need this in the afterlife. I'll have armour to wear now.'

The afterlife! Jumping Jupiter . . . Lucius!

Felix turned around and ran back to where Missy leaned over Lucius.

'The bleeding's slowing down, and he's still breathing,' she said, without looking up.

'We need to get him somewhere safe,' Felix said. 'Help us!' Some of the others ran over, and between them they lifted Lucius up into the air. The crowd cheered and clapped as Lucius was carried out of the arena.

They went as quickly as they could back to the school, but by the time they got there Lucius was unconscious.

'We should take him to the doctor's hut,' suggested Livia.

'So we can be told to sacrifice a chicken and hope for the best?' Felix said. 'I don't think so.'

'Do you think he'll need surgery?' Missy asked. 'To remove the arrowhead? We could take him back home with us – the doctors there could save him.'

Felix frowned and shook his head. 'We have to save him here. And we *can* save him. If the bleeding has stopped then hopefully the arrowhead missed his artery. But I don't want to risk it and remove the arrow in case he bleeds to death. The best thing we can do is leave it in there and hope that the wound heals and doesn't become infected.'

* * *

The next few days passed by like a strange dream. Lucius flitted in and out of consciousness, speaking nonsense about his family and about moving away to run his own farm every time he woke up. Felix and Missy kept his wound clean by washing it with cooled boiled water and using as many natural resources as they could find . . .

Natural antiseptics:

* Honey
* Lemon
* Tea tree oil
* Lavender

Natural antibiotics (to kill off infection):

* Carob powder
* Colloidal silver

Lucius was asleep on the day Felix and Missy had a visitor.

'Attilia!' they called out, greeting the former gladiator warmly. She wore a woman's toga, and in her strong arms she carried a brown sack, her weapons and her armour, including her amazing golden helmet.

'I've come to say thank you and goodbye. I'm leaving Rome – there are too many bad memories for me here. I'm taking a small part of the fortune Nero gave me along with my freedom, and I'm going back home.'

'What about the rest of your fortune?' Missy asked. 'What will you do with that?'

Attilia knelt down before them and bowed her head. 'These are yours now.' She laid the golden helmet, the armour, the weapons and the sack – which jingled with gold coins – at Felix's feet. 'You are the one who won me my freedom. These belong to you. I have no need of them now.'

'I have no need of them either,' Felix replied, bemused.

Attilia smiled. 'Then use that wise head of yours to give them to someone who does.' Attilia saluted Felix and Missy. 'For the glory of the Empire!'

'For the glory of the Empire!' they saluted her back.

* * *

Lucius finally woke up a whole week after they had fought and won in the arena. His cheeks were rosy and his strength seemed to have returned. 'I had the strangest dreams,' he told Felix and Missy. 'I dreamed that I was a farmer, and I had a hundred pigs and goats and cows and sheep.'

'Maybe the gods were showing you the future?' Missy smiled at him.

'Lucius,' Felix said seriously, 'all these things . . .' He pointed to the helmet, the armour, the weapons and the fortune of gold coins. 'I can't take them back with me. I don't want to. I want you to have them.'

'But, Felix, I can't—' Lucius began to protest.

'Yes, you can,' Felix said firmly. 'And you will. You've always dreamed of being a farmer. Take the money and use it to get as far away from Rome as you can. Buy a farm. Buy some animals. Grow old and be happy. You deserve it.'

'How can I ever thank you?' Lucius replied quietly.

Felix smiled and looked at Missy. 'You don't need to thank us. Just promise you'll never forget us.'

Lucius picked up the gleaming golden helmet and inspected it, wide-eyed. 'I don't know what I'll do with this. I don't ever want to fight again. Maybe I'll ask to be buried in it! Who knows . . . But, Felix, will you do something for me?'

'Anything.'

Lucius pointed at Felix's bag. 'The knife you carry around. Can you use it to carve your name into this helmet? That way, every time I look at it, I'll think of you.'

* * *

Felix woke up the next morning with Einstein pulling on his ear.

He rubbed his eyes and watched as the little lizard crawled down his arm and on to the bed.

There was a letter at the end of the mattress, addressed to 'Felix and Missy'.

Felix picked up the letter, dragged himself out of bed and tiptoed towards Missy. He prodded her until she woke up. 'Look – let's read this.'

Dear Felix and Missy,

I hope you don't think that not saying goodbye means that I don't care. In fact it means the opposite. How can I ever tell you to your faces just how much meeting you has meant to me? How can I ever put into words all the things I'm thankful for ...?

Thank you for teaching me to fight.

Thank you for teaching me how to be brave.

Thank you for making me a pair of glasses so I can see the world in all its beauty.

Thank you for showing me the importance of teamwork.

Thank you for saving my life.

Thank you for giving me the means to leave Rome and start a new life.

Thank you for everything.

I'm leaving Rome before the sun rises, before you wake up. I'm going to see my family first. I hope they will want me back – but if they don't then I plan to get as far away from Rome as possible.

Have you heard of Britannia? It's a small island at the edge of the Roman Empire. The weather is dreadful, and the people are savages, but the fortune you have given me will buy me a farm and a new life there.

I've left you half of the gold coins. I know you said you don't need them, but I couldn't leave you with nothing.

Now that I am free, I hope that I live a full and happy life, and die a contented old man. And I meant what I said about Attilia's armour – one day, when I'm old and grey and surrounded by my great-grandchildren, then I'm going to be buried in it.

May the gods keep you safe on all your adventures to come.

For the glory of the Empire.

Your friend,

Lucius

18
Professor Aldini

'Sherlock Holmes said, "When you eliminate the impossible, whatever remains, however improbable, must be the truth."'

Felix fastened his backpack and swung it over his shoulders. He began to tap in the co-ordinates for home into the old TV remote control. Einstein crawled into his pocket, turning **green** at the thought of the stomach-flipping time travelling they were about to do.

After Lucius had left Rome, Felix and Missy had spent another day at the school. They'd changed a couple of the gold coins into smaller currency so they could give all of the children there enough money to enrol in proper schools.

'I know,' Missy said to Felix, putting on her own backpack. 'But do you really think it's true? Lucius is the skeleton in the garden?'

'Of course it's true.' Felix's finger hovered over the green button. 'All the facts are there.'

The facts:

❋ *Lucius has an arrowhead embedded in his chest. The skeleton in the garden wasn't murdered – the arrowhead had been there for years before he died.*

❋ *The helmet, armour, golden coins, ring, glasses and belt buckle buried with the skeleton all belonged to Lucius.*

'Mystery solved,' said Felix. 'Just call me **Felix Frost: Time Detective.**'

'Hey, that sounds quite cool.' Missy smiled at him, bracing herself for the journey home. 'Maybe we could set up some kind of bureau of investigation. We could go through the history books and find the greatest mysteries of all time, then we could fire up the old microwave and solve—'

Felix pressed down on the green button

before Missy finished speaking and they began hurtling through space and time. Felix felt his skin ripple and hum with energy, his atoms pull apart and then ping back together in the space of a nanosecond.

In the blink of an eye they were standing in Felix's bedroom. It was just as they'd left it: the walls covered with scientific equations, stacks of well-thumbed physics books piled high on the bookshelves and the funny stench of the mould jar creeping up Felix's nose.

Darwin's beard — it's good to be home! thought Felix.

Before he could even take his backpack off, his bedroom door swung open and his brother Frank walked in. 'Er, Felix, have you finally lost it, or what?' In his hand was the letter Felix had written to his family, over two months ago. The letter that explained he was about to travel back in time.

'Ha ha!' Felix snatched the note out of Frank's hands. 'It's a joke – funny, huh?'

Frank looked at Felix as though he were covered from head to toe in green slime. 'I swear your hair's longer than it was at dinner time. You're such a weirdo. How are we related . . .?' He walked out without another word, and without bothering to shut the door behind him.

'We need to get back to the museum,' Missy said quickly. 'Before they realize things are missing.'

* * *

The museum was closed when Missy and Felix arrived back in London that evening. Missy had a key to the staff door, and she let them in and tapped in the security code so the alarms didn't sound.

'It feels like a lifetime ago since we were last here,' Missy said to Felix, leading him up a back staircase towards the room that Lucius's skeleton was being kept in. 'Not this morning.'

'Well, time might not have changed here, but more than two months have passed for us,' Felix pointed out.

'Does that mean I'm two months closer to my next birthday but I STILL have to wait another six months to celebrate it?' Missy frowned.

'Yes, it certainly does pose some interesting

scientific questions,' Felix mused. 'Maybe I'll run some equations, tally up some stats and see—'

'Missy,' came a voice behind them.

They were outside the small, dusty room where all the hidden Roman artefacts were being kept, and Missy was just about to turn the handle.

'Professor Aldini,' Missy said, turning around and addressing the man who had followed them up the stairs. She shifted uneasily from side to side, her lips twitching. 'I was just . . . just . . .'

'Talking utter nonsense with your friend here,' the man said wryly, looking Felix up and down. He was tall and slim with slicked-over black hair and large round glasses obscuring his dark eyes. He wore a threadbare suit and a stiff-collared shirt.

So this is what he looks like — the guy who threatened Missy's mum.
Nano-brain.

'I'm Professor Aldini,' the man said to Felix, without asking who he was or offering him a handshake in greeting. 'I assume you have permission to be in the museum outside opening hours.'

'You assume correctly, professor,' Missy replied.

He stared at her intently for a moment. 'Tell your mother that if she hasn't solved the mystery of the skeleton in the garden by next week then she shouldn't bother coming back to work.' Professor Aldini turned and scuttled down the stairs without another word.

'Well that was as pleasant as standing in a meteor shower without an umbrella.' Felix laughed sarcastically.

'I hate him!' Missy said, turning the handle and pushing the door open. She fumbled around for the light switch. 'He's so creepy. And I don't trust him at all. I don't know why – maybe it's because—'

'Because he just threatened your mum's job?' Felix suggested. 'Don't worry – your mum will be the one who solves the mystery of the century and that idiot will have to eat his slimy words.'

They fell silent as the old strip lights above them zinged to life.

The table in the middle of the room was just how it had been before.

In the centre were the bleached bones of the Roman man, surrounded by Attilia's armour, weapons and brilliant golden helmet.

'I guess I should return these,' Missy said, pulling out the ring, buckle and broken glasses from her bag. 'And these . . .' She emptied out the gold coins that Lucius had given them – luckily just enough to replace the ones Missy had taken and spent back in Ancient Rome.

'He must have led a good life you know.' Felix smiled, feeling slightly strange that he was looking down at Lucius's skeleton. 'He lived to an old age – and all his old battle wounds and the arrowhead in his chest obviously never held him back.'

'Thank you for letting me tag along on the adventure, Felix,' Missy said quietly.

'I didn't have much choice,' he replied. 'You hitched a lift, remember?'

'Felix?'

'Yes?'

'Are you going to tell anyone else about this? About the time machine and—'

'No!' Felix said firmly. 'No one must ever know.'

'I suppose a time machine in the wrong hands would be a disaster,' Missy said thoughtfully. 'How about that brain of yours? Are you ever going to tell anyone about that?'

'No. And you can't tell anyone either – you promised.'

'I did,' Missy agreed. 'But you know what you promised me? You have to join the school science club.'

'Ugh!' Felix let out a sigh. 'Fine, whatever!'

Missy smiled to herself. 'And you have to let me come along whenever you next time travel.'

'What makes you think I want to go time travelling ever again?' Felix asked, alarmed.

'Because you're **Felix Frost: Time Detective**,' Missy told him.

I am, he thought. *I have a time machine at my fingertips and the whole of human history to explore . . . Where shall I go next?*

SKELETON IN THE GARDEN – UNEARTHED

Today sees the publication of Professor Debbie Six's paper, 'The Skeleton in the Garden'. The paper details the remarkable discovery regarding the identity of the Roman skeleton that was recently unearthed in a suburban garden.

'The murder mystery is not a murder mystery at all,' said Professor Debbie Six, head of Roman artefacts at the British Museum.

'Further tests have revealed that the mysterious skeleton in the garden was once a man aged between seventy and seventy-five years old. A very elderly man in Roman terms,' confirmed Professor Six. 'The wounds that we initially discovered on his body – the fractured leg and the arrowhead imbedded in his chest – appear to have been sustained when he was a child. Remarkably, these wounds healed well at the time they were inflicted, and the man lived to an elderly age.

'We managed to trace his sealstone ring back to a farming family who lived just outside Rome during Emperor Nero's reign. Records show that the family sold their youngest son, Lucius, into a gladiator school when he was just a boy. After Lucius won his freedom, he left Rome and disappeared from all records. No one knew what happened to him, until now. We know he was greatly loved and revered by his community. And this find remains one of the most important Roman discoveries in this country to date.

'History is full of unsolved mysteries, and while we now know as much as we ever will about the skeleton in the garden, we may never know all the answers to our questions. If only we had a time machine,' laughed Professor Six. 'Then we'd have all the answers.'

Felix, Missy & Einstein
return in

Felix Frost
Time Detective

GHOST
PLANE

JANUARY 2016

History just
got real!

www.quercusbooks.co.uk

Quercus